Penina Levine

Is a Hard-Boiled Egg

Penina Levine

Is a Hard-Boiled Egg

Rebecca O'Connell

ILLUSTRATED BY Majella Lue Sue

A DEBORAH BRODIE BOOK
ROARING BROOK PRESS
NEW MILFORD, CONNECTICUT

A Deborah Brodie Book
Published by Roaring Brook Press
Roaring Brook Press is a division of Holtzbrinck Publishing Holdings Limited
Partnership
143 West Street, New Milford, Connecticut 06776

Library of Congress Cataloging-in-Publication Data
O'Connell, Rebecca, 1968-
Penina Levine is a hard-boiled egg / by Rebecca O'Connell ;
illustrated by Majella Lue Sue. — 1st ed.
p. cm.
"A Deborah Brodie book."
Summary: With only her best friend to lean on, forthright Penina
celebrates Passover while she contends with a bratty younger sister
and a seemingly unsympathetic sixth-grade teacher.
ISBN-13: 978-1-59643-140-9   ISBN-10: 1-59643-140-7
[1. Best friends—Fiction.. 2. Friendship—Fiction. 3. Schools—Fiction.
4. Jews—Fiction. 5. Passover—Fiction.]   I. Lue Sue, Majella, ill.   II. Title.
PZ7.O2167Pen 2007   [Fic]—dc22
2006016677

Book design by Jennifer Browne
Printed in the United States of America
First edition March 2007
2   4   6   8   10   9   7   5   3   1

To Cathy DeRaleau

Contents

Check-Out Receipt

Alameda Free Library
Main Branch
1550 Oak Street
Alameda, CA 94501
Tel: 510-747-7777
www.alamedafree.org
Checkout Date: 04-10-2016 - 14:09:13

Patron ID.: xxxxxxxxxx3071

---

1 Scary stories 3 : more tales to chill y
33341003871638   **DueDate:** 05/01/16

2 Penina Levine is a hard-boiled egg /
33341007173312   **DueDate:** 05/01/16

3 Dress-up mess-up /
33341005457642   **DueDate:** 05/01/16

4 Pinkalicious : cherry blossom /
33341005591739   **DueDate:** 05/01/16

5 Emma's strange pet /
33341004283320   **DueDate:** 05/01/16

6 Amelia Bedelia sleeps over /
33341007831992   **DueDate:** 05/01/16

7 The secret history /
33341002001955   **DueDate:** 05/01/16

Total Items: 7

Balance Due: $ 2.10

**Effective July 8: Main Branch will open
at 10AM on Wed**

1. Shut Up

Shut up, Mimsy!

Penina thought it. Inside her head, she shouted it, stood up on the dinner table and bellowed it until her sister stopped chattering, singing, rhyming, and humming. She imagined a world without Mimsy's nonstop noise.

But *shut up* was not allowed. *Shut up* had earned Penina more days of being grounded than there were green beans piled on her plate.

"Henin!" yelled Mimsy. "Henny-wenny-benny henin!" She took off her pointy pink princess hat and put it on the table. The trailing scarf landed in a bowl of applesauce. That kind of hat was called a henin. Their dad knew a lot about historical stuff, and he had told Mimsy her hat was a henin.

Penina's hat, really. It had been in Penina's dress-up bin, but since she didn't play dress-up anymore, and since Mimsy was a nosy little snoop who went through other people's things, and since Mom and

Dad let Mimsy have whatever she wanted, the henin now belonged to Mimsy.

"The royal henin of Her Highness, Princess Mimsy-kins!" Mimsy announced.

Penina put her hands over her ears. "Mimsy!" she shouted. She almost said, "shut up," but she stopped herself in time. Instead, she said, "Look at this."

She took a coin from her pocket and held it up for everyone to see. It was bigger than a quarter, and it gleamed with a golden glow. On its face, a smiling young woman with a baby on her back peered over her shoulder at Penina.

"It's a Sacagawea dollar," said Mom.

"Where'd you get that?" asked Dad.

"I got it in change at the Maple Street Market," said Penina. She and Zozo sometimes stopped there after school. "And, Mimsy, you can have it"—Mimsy grabbed for the coin, but Penina jerked it out of her reach—"*if* you can do one thing."

"I can do it," said Mimsy. "I can jump down four steps without falling, and I can wink one eye." Mimsy closed her eyes and opened them one at a time. "See?"

Mom and Dad oohed and ahhed over Mimsy's remarkable ability to open her eyes. Penina waited it out. She breathed on Sacajawea and shined her up with a paper napkin.

"Give me it!" yelled Mimsy.

2

"Not yet," said Penina. "I will give you this gen-
uine 2001 United States Sacagawea one-dollar coin
if you, Mimsy Levine, can be quiet for ten whole
minutes."

"Okay," said Mimsy. She put on her henin and
leaned back in her chair.

"Come on, Penina," said Dad.

"That's not fair," said Mom. "She's only four. She
can't stay quiet for ten minutes."

"Shh. You'll ruin it," Penina said. She took a bite
of green beans. She could actually hear herself chew-
ing them.

"She doesn't know what ten minutes is," Dad protested.

"I do so!" yelled Mimsy. She sat up suddenly, knocking her henin to the floor. Her hair made a swirly brown cloud around her head. It sproinged all over the place unless it was trapped beneath a henin or something. Penina's was the same way. She always kept her curls contained in braids or a ponytail.

"I should have known you couldn't do it," Penina muttered. She put Sacagawea away. Too bad. She would have been happy to trade it for ten minutes of Mimsy's silence.

"That doesn't count! I was talking to Daddy!" Mimsy screamed.

"Yes, it counts. The deal was you had to be quiet for ten minutes. You couldn't even be quiet for thirty seconds."

"That's not fair!" screamed Mimsy.

"That's not fair," Dad remarked.

"Why not let her try again, Pen?" Mom suggested.

"No. Why bother? She'll just do the same thing all over again. She doesn't know how to stop talking. Nothing in the world can make Mimsy shut up!"

Except, of course, for Penina getting into trouble. That was one thing that could make Mimsy sit still and listen. When Penina said "shut up," Mimsy's eyes opened wide. She snapped her head around to stare

4

at Penina. Mom gasped. Dad put down his water glass with extreme care.

"Penina," he said slowly. He almost sighed it.

Penina stared at her plate. Only a few green beans left. She had already eaten all her applesauce. She hadn't touched her chicken. She didn't like the kind with spicy coating.

"Tell Mimsy you're sorry," Mom ordered.

Penina lifted her eyes, but not her head. Mimsy shrugged one shoulder and tilted her head, her cuteness routine. Grown-ups loved it, but Penina knew it was totally fake. Mimsy was about as cute as a Burmese python, a vampire bat, a deep-sea tube worm.

"It's okay, Pina," Mimsy said, "I still love you."

"Well, I hate you!" Penina screamed. She slammed down her spoon and pushed back her chair.

"I hate you!" she screamed again. She was bigger than Mimsy, and she could be louder, too. Her scream could break all the glasses on the table, bend the forks and spoons, push all the dishes onto the floor. "I. Hate. You!" she screamed, and before she got the last word out, she turned and ran out of the kitchen, up the stairs, and into her room.

She couldn't *stand* Mimsy. Everyone thought Mimsy was so cute, but all she ever did was get Penina in trouble.

2. A Friendly Letter

"I can't. I'm grounded," Penina whispered.

"Why?" Zozo whispered back. Neither girl looked at the other. They kept their eyes straight ahead. Ms. Anderson might hear murmuring, but she wouldn't be able to tell who was doing it.

"Because Mimsy is a crybaby and a tattletale," Penina answered.

"Focus, people," Ms. Anderson said. "Let's have less talk, more work."

She reminded Penina of a pony: short and strong and sturdy. Penina thought of the pink and pale blue toy ponies she played with when she was little. It was weird. If only Ms. Anderson had a wavy purple tail, she would look just like Pansy Pony, brought to life.

Zozo smiled up at Ms. Anderson and fluttered her eyelashes. *I wasn't whispering. I was paying attention. I am an excellent student.* That always worked for Zozo.

Ms. Anderson looked at Penina, and Penina

6

looked down and concentrated on her pencil. It was covered in bite marks. She loved the way it crunched when she pressed her teeth into it.

"All right," Ms. Anderson continued. "Today we start something new." She was passing out a stack of colored paper.

Zozo got hers first. "Oh, you're going to *love* this," Zozo whispered, and Penina could tell she meant "you're going to hate this."

On the paper was the outline of a rabbit's head, with lines for writing where the face would have been. Above the long ears were the words—underlined about six times—GREETINGS FROM THE EASTER BUNNY!

Zozo was right. Penina did hate this. She hated it when Ms. Anderson made them do stupid stuff. Like the Reading Olympics. Ms. Anderson had said that whatever team read the most would win a pizza party. Penina read. She read every day. She read thick books. But her team didn't win. Ms. Anderson counted the number of books, not the number of pages or time spent reading or whether the books were good, sixth-grade-level books or stupid skinny books for babies.

Ms. Anderson passed Penina's desk and put down a pale yellow paper. She said, "My friend, Ms. Stewart, teaches kindergarten at Holy Family School, and we're going to create individualized Easter greetings for her students!"

Everyone got a folded-up letter from a kindergartener. Penina smoothed hers out on the desk. It was that lined beige paper with the really wide spaces, the kind for little kids to practice writing on. But the writing wasn't little-kid writing. It was the neatest writing Penina had ever seen.

Dear Easter Bunny,
    Please bring me a big chocolate rabbit and a bag of jelly dino eggs.
        Happy Easter.
            Love,
                Alan

"Now you can *be* the Easter Bunny," said Ms. Anderson. "You can make this a magical Easter for a little girl or boy. How cool is that?"

Not cool at all. Penina leaned over and whispered to Zozo, "How dumb is that?"

"Penina, do you have something to say?" Ms. Anderson asked.

"No," Penina said. This was worse than the Reading Olympics.

"Now, we're going to have fun with this," said Ms. Anderson.

8

Penina groaned. Mrs. Brown had never made them do anything like this. Ms. Anderson had been teaching them only since January, when their real teacher, Mrs. Brown, had moved to Arizona. Penina missed her.

"Penina, is there a problem?" asked Ms. Anderson.

Penina couldn't do an assignment about Easter. Her family didn't celebrate it, and she would feel weird pretending that she did. "We don't celebrate Easter," Penina said.

She put her pencil in her mouth, but took it right back out. She'd chew on it later, when everyone wasn't staring at her.

"That's okay," Ms. Anderson said. "You can still write the letter. Use your imagination."

This had nothing to do with imagination. Penina had a good imagination. Right now she was imagining herself getting up, walking out of the classroom, and spending the rest of the day at the mall.

Zozo raised her hand. "Ms. Anderson, Penina doesn't have the Easter Bunny. She's Jewish."

Penina gave Zozo a look: *Thank you.*

Zozo looked back: *No problem.*

"I understand that," said Ms. Anderson. "But she can still do the assignment."

Penina didn't want to do the assignment. Easter was not her holiday. She did not believe in a giant

9

egg-laying rabbit, and she did not see why she should pretend she did. Penina traced the rabbit-head outline with her finger. It was like the work sheet was a coded message, and the message was, *We all celebrate this holiday with bunnies and jelly beans and chocolate eggs. Everyone in this class does.*

Penina picked up the letter from Alan. He had drawn a lopsided rabbit and a mound of colored blobs beneath the message. Poor kid. He was probably just hoping for something good in his Easter basket. She'd just write him a nice, normal note. Maybe she'd put in a knock-knock joke or something. Mimsy loved knock-knock jokes, and Alan wasn't much older than Mimsy.

Penina put her name and *Marionville School* at the top of the rabbit page, and the date below that. She knew how to set up a friendly letter. They'd done it in fourth grade.

Dear Alan, she wrote. She made the *A* straight and tall.

"Who is writing this letter?"

Penina jumped. She hadn't seen the teacher come to stand by her desk.

"Me?" Penina guessed. She looked at Zozo.

Zozo's look said *Uh-oh.*

"This is true," said Ms. Anderson, "but you're writing it *as* the Easter Bunny. So, there's no reason

10

for you to put your name at the top of the page."

Ms. Anderson took another piece of bunny-head paper from the stack on her desk and brought it to Penina. "You can start over. We will be sharing these with Ms. Stewart's class, and we don't want to send them something with eraser marks."

Penina took the paper, but she didn't say anything. She didn't write anything, either.

"Go for it, Penina." Ms. Anderson tapped Penina's blank page. "Pencil to paper."

"I don't believe in the Easter Bunny," said Penina.

"Got it," Ms. Anderson said. "But the kindergartener who wrote to you does. That's why your letter will mean so much to him. Besides, it's creative writing. That means you can make stuff up. Have fun with it!"

No fun. This letter was not fun, and it wasn't creative, either. If Penina could have decided for herself what to write, *that* would have been creative. Penina would have made up a great story for Alan. It would have been a story about gnomes and elves and talking horses and flying monkeys, and it would have been better than an Easter Bunny letter, because Penina could have really put her heart into it.

"I'm not going to pretend to be the Easter Bunny," Penina said. "It's against my beliefs."

"Ooooh!" went everybody in the class. They

made it low and spooky. Penina was in trouble.

Zozo gave her a look like, *Are you really going to make a big deal out of this?*

Yes. It was a big deal. Penina did not celebrate Easter. It wasn't fair for Ms. Anderson to assume that everyone in the whole entire world grew up believing in the Easter Bunny. As if everyone should. As if Penina didn't count.

"What about Ryan?" said someone in the back. "He's Jewish. Does he have to write the letter?"

Everyone looked at Penina and Ryan. Penina and Ryan looked at each other.

Penina guessed she and Ryan were friends, but outside temple and religious school, they didn't spend much time together. He sat with the boys who all went to soccer and basketball camp together, and she always sat with Zozo. He was friendly, though, and his curly orange hair reminded Penina of marigolds.

"Ryan," said Ms. Anderson, "are you okay with this assignment?"

Penina saw the blush rush from Ryan's neck all the way up to his forehead. "I don't know," he said.

Come on, Ryan, thought Penina, tell her!

"Do you understand why I'm asking you to do this assignment with the rest of the class?" Ms. Anderson asked him.

"I guess so," said Ryan. He was so red he matched the stripes on the flag above Ms. Anderson's desk.

He didn't care. He didn't mind. He didn't get it. Nobody got it. It wasn't fair.

"Good," she said. "How about you, Penina? Are we cool?"

Oh, no. Penina felt an ache in her forehead, a tickle in her nose. She knew the feeling. She was going to cry. No matter what she did now, there was no way to stop it.

"Penina?" Ms. Anderson asked softly. "Did you hear me?"

Penina nodded. Her nose was already dripping, and she didn't have a tissue. She sniffled. She had to. It was that or drip nose-goo onto her desk. Then the tears came.

"Oh, Penina!" said Ms. Anderson. That's what her words said. Her voice said, *Oh, come on! There's nothing to cry about.*

"Zozo," Ms. Anderson said, "please walk Penina to the girls' room and help her wash her face."

"I can wash my face by myself!" Penina yelled. She ran into the hallway.

3. Stupid, Stupid, Stupid

Penina boosted herself up and sat on the edge of the sink. There was nowhere else to sit. The toilets in the girls' room didn't have lids.

Her rabbit head stationery had a hole in it. Her finger had punched right through the bunny's right ear when she crumpled up the paper. That was too bad. She didn't have anything against the Easter Bunny. She didn't have anything against Easter. Penina had dyed eggs with Zozo before, and she was a big fan of those yellow marshmallow chicks. *Those* were Easter things, and she didn't feel weird about them. But this was different. This was an assignment. This was for a grade. She had to write as the Easter Bunny whether she liked it or not.

She blew her nose in a paper towel and threw it at the wastebasket. It missed.

She got down and picked up the crumpled towel. She threw it, hard, into the wastebasket. Stupid towel.

Stupid wastebasket. She kicked it. Stupid plastic. It didn't even make a noise. Metal wastebaskets were a lot better for kicking.

Stupid shoes. She couldn't kick a wastebasket in shoes that gave her blisters. They were new. They were just like Zozo's, and they were too tight. She couldn't help it if she'd grown in the last week and a half since she and Mom had gone shopping. The shoes were killing her feet.

It was too bad, because the shoes looked good with the dress she had on, one of her Naomi dresses.

Naomi was Penina's cousin. Penina knew that if they lived closer, they would be best friends. Naomi was only ten, but she could already read Hebrew. She knew French, too. They taught it at her school. She could play piano, and she knew how to ski. She was taller than Penina, even though she was younger, and Penina sometimes got her hand-me-down dresses. They were her favorite clothes.

She'd see Naomi soon. Penina's family always went to Grandma and Grandpa's house in Peekskill for the Seder, and Naomi was always there. She couldn't wait. She'd tell Naomi all about the stupid letter, stupid wastebasket, stupid shoes. When she told Naomi, she'd find a way to make the whole thing sound funny, but for now, it was anything but. She blew her nose again and threw away the towel.

She dropped the crumpled yellow rabbit paper into the toilet bowl.

The bathroom door opened, and Zozo walked in.

"Come on," she said. "It's almost lunchtime. I'm supposed to get you and bring you to the cafeteria." She handed Penina a purple insulated lunch bag with a chimpanzee key chain clipped to the zipper. Zozo's looked just like it, but with a tiger.

"Thanks," said Penina. Penina and Zozo never bought lunch in the cafeteria. Zozo had about a million food allergies and had to be really careful about what she ate. Penina just thought cafeteria food was gross.

They were the first ones in the cafeteria, so they got the big round table by the window. They could see the whole room from there. Penina watched the lunch line, and when she saw Ryan standing in it, she got up and walked over.

"Hi," she said.

"Hi," he said, and stepped back so she could get in line in front of him.

"Oh, no, thanks," she said, "I brought my lunch."

"Hey! No cutting!" said Jesse, two back in line from Ryan.

Ryan turned around to look at Jesse, but kept his

foot in line to hold his place. "She's not cutting, you dingleberry!"

Jesse made a face, but he didn't say anything else, and Ryan got back in line. "Sorry about all that Easter Bunny stuff," he said. "I just figured, might as well write the letter and get it over with."

"That's okay," said Penina. "What did you write?"

Ryan smiled. His top middle teeth were bigger than the others. It made *him* look a little like the

Easter Bunny. "I told him the key to finding the most eggs was to get down low and look around the edges of the yard."

Penina stared at him. "But why?"

"Because it took me years to figure that out. I wish someone had clued me in when I was five."

"But you're Jewish!" Penina said. She almost shouted it.

Ryan shrugged. "Yeah, but my dad is Catholic. We

always have an Easter egg hunt at my uncle's house."

"Oh," said Penina. "I don't like Ms. Anderson. I told her I don't believe in the Easter Bunny."

Ryan shrugged again. "It's just for fun," he said.

"But it's the *Easter* Bunny, and it's not fair. We didn't try to make the whole class pretend to be King Ahasuerus!"

Ryan laughed. He'd dressed up as King Ahasuerus for the temple Purim party a few weeks ago. "Yeah, well, but the Easter Bunny isn't religious or anything."

"Yes it is!" Penina said. "It's not called the *Springtime Bunny* or the *Candy Egg Bunny*. It's the *Easter* Bunny, and Easter is a religious holiday."

"I just don't think it's that big a deal," said Ryan. "So what if I write an Easter Bunny letter? I'm still Jewish."

Well, duh. Doing the Easter Bunny assignment wasn't going to suddenly change her. That wasn't what she meant. It wasn't fair of Ms. Anderson to make them pretend to be the Easter Bunny, and it wasn't fair of her to make Penina explain why it wasn't fair.

"Hey, Levine, you're holding up the line!" Jesse yelled from behind Ryan and Suzie.

Penina realized the line had moved up, but she

and Ryan hadn't. She stepped out of the way, and Ryan grabbed his tray and silverware.

"Okay, bye," said Penina. She started to go. Zozo was waving to her from the big table.

"Hey, wait," said Ryan. "Don't you still have to write the Easter Bunny letter?"

Some little kid—Alan—was waiting for an answer from the Easter Bunny. Whoever Alan was, it wasn't his fault their teachers had thought up this stupid assignment. She would write him a letter, but not as the Easter Bunny. She would write as herself—on regular white notebook paper. Penina thought about the pale yellow page from Ms. Anderson swishing around and around the toilet bowl in the girls' room before it disappeared forever.

"No," she said, "I don't."

4. No One Listens

"Of course, you still do have to write the letter," Ms. Anderson said. She leaned down and rested her palms on Penina's desk. She smelled like wintergreen gum. "You can do it at home, since you didn't finish it in class."

"I can't," said Penina. The wintergreen smell was suffocating her.

"Now, Penina, what do I always say about that word?"

Penina recited, "*Can't* is a four-letter word."

"That's right," Ms. Anderson said, and stepped back. Penina could breathe again.

"I don't have the paper," she said.

"Then here's a replacement," said Ms. Anderson. She laid a pastel yellow sheet of paper on Penina's desk. Penina put it in her take-home folder. Later, she stuffed the take-home folder in her backpack, slung her backpack over her shoulder, hauled it home, and dropped it on the floor in the kitchen.

22

"You're not allowed to leave that there!" yelled Mimsy. "Mom! Penina left her backpack on the floor again."

Penina made a face at her sister and kicked her backpack into the closet. Mimsy made a face back, so Penina took off Mimsy's pointy pink princess hat, with the dried applesauce on the scarf, and threw it into the basement.

"M-o-m!" Mimsy screamed, like a fire alarm, like a police siren, like the emergency-drill bell at school.

Mom's office was in the attic. Penina heard her mother hurry down the stairs. She jumped over the last three and skidded into the kitchen.

"What is it? Mimsy, are you all right?" Mom put her arm around Mimsy and stroked her hair. "Penina, what happened?"

"Nothing," said Penina.

At the same time, Mimsy said, "She threw my henin in the basement."

Mom opened the door to the basement, pointed down the steps, and told Penina, "Go get it."

She did. She brought it up. She had her snack. She went to her room. She didn't say anything about the Easter Bunny letter. Why should she? No one listened to her anyway.

5. Barb and Barbara

"I can't. I told you, I'm grounded." Penina switched the phone to her other ear. Next door, in the Millers' living room, Zozo switched her phone to her other ear, too. Penina saw her do it through the window. They liked to talk on the phone watching each other. It was like having a giant video-phone. They called it the Window Phone.

The Window Phone window had long drapes for Penina to hide behind while she talked. If she whispered, no one in her house even knew she wasn't up in her room, being grounded.

"You're always grounded," Zozo said. "Does your sister tell on you for just basically existing?"

"Pretty much," said Penina.

Zozo shook her head. She had a hairdo for every day of the week. Today was Tuesday, so at school Zozo's shiny black hair had been in two smooth braids with matching elastics. Yesterday had been one braid in the back, and tomorrow would be a ponytail. After that, two ponytails, one 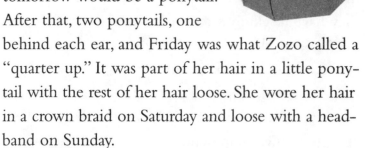 behind each ear, and Friday was what Zozo called a "quarter up." It was part of her hair in a little ponytail with the rest of her hair loose. She wore her hair in a crown braid on Saturday and loose with a headband on Sunday.

"Not fair," said Zozo. "But they can't stop you from going into your own yard, can they? Just stay on your side of the property line, and I'll stay on mine. You won't technically be breaking the law."

"Okay," said Penina. She knew it wasn't fair for her to play with Zozo if she was supposed to be grounded, but it wasn't fair for her to be grounded in the first place, so she thought it evened out.

Penina didn't have to ask what Zozo wanted to do. When they met in their backyards, they almost always brought Barb and Barbara. Barb and Barbara were fashion dolls. Penina and Zozo didn't talk about them at school. Everyone else had quit dressing up dolls in second grade, but Penina and Zozo didn't use them for dress-up. They set up a campsite for them in the backyard and made Barb and Barbara into naturalists collecting data in a remote wilderness outpost.

"Let's pretend the blue spruce tree is a giant mountain, and there's an eagle's nest at the top, and they have to climb it to count the eggs," said Zozo.

"No, the blue spruce is way over in your yard. I can't go there," said Penina.

"Okay, well, then, let's pretend that just Barbara is climbing the mountain, and Barb has to stay here and guard the equipment."

"Yeah. Barb is running experiments at camp, but it's really dangerous, because the giant prowler is stalking around the area." Penina pointed at Daisy, her calico cat, dozing on the back porch.

Zozo helped Barbara put on her homemade knapsack and hiking boots. "And it's a really dangerous climb for Barbara alone, but Barb can't go because of her religion."

"What?" Penina quit arranging the dolls' campsite and looked at Zozo. "Why would mountain climbing be against Barb's religion?"

26

"I don't know. Everything else is."

"What are you talking about, Zozo?"

"Well, Barb is Jewish, right?"

"I guess so."

"Then she's not allowed to eat cheeseburgers or cut paper snowflakes or write Easter letters."

Penina stared at Zozo, and then at Barb and Barbara. They all had dark hair. Most of the fashion dolls had blond hair, but Penina and Zozo liked the brunette dolls. They liked being a little different. Penina was the only Jewish girl in their class. Zozo was the only kid in the whole school whose grandfather had come from Iran. She was the only one who stood up for Penina when Ms. Anderson gave them that letter.

Penina couldn't even think about all the different ways Zozo wasn't making sense right now. All she could say was, "Jews can so make snowflakes."

"No, they can't. Snowflakes are for Christmas, like bunnies are for Easter," Zozo said. She hugged Barbara to her chest.

Penina twirled her finger in Barb's hair. "Zozo, we made a paper blizzard last year. We decorated the snowflakes with silver glitter-glue. Don't you remember?"

"Tsk." Zozo clicked her tongue. "Well, then, why couldn't you just write the stupid Easter Bunny letter like everybody else?"

"It's not the same thing!" Penina yelled. Was Zozo serious? She really couldn't see the difference between the Easter Bunny letter and the paper snowflakes?

"First of all"—Penina pulled her finger out of Barb's hair and used it to count—"I wanted to cut out the snowflakes, not like the Easter Bunny letter, where I was forced. Second of all"—she stuck out another finger—"snowflakes aren't against my religion. I can cut out as many snowflakes as I want without breaking Jewish law."

"Well, you do have a lot of weird laws," Zozo said, but she was smiling. "We do, too. Like, no meat on Fridays for six weeks before Easter. If I have to eat one more fish stick, I'm going to grow gills and fins." She made a silly fish-face. "When you think about it, everyone's religion is a little weird."

She smiled again and fluttered her eyelashes until Penina had to smile too. It wasn't just for teachers, that fluttering. This time the flutters said, *Sorry. I crossed a line. Don't be angry.*

How did Zozo do that? Penina spent about half their time together being mad at Zozo, but Zozo always made Penina want to be her friend again.

"Come in for a second. I want to show you my Easter basket."

"You got it already?" Easter wasn't for a while yet.

28

"No, I mean the one I'm making for my mom. It's almost done. You have to see it."

"Zozo, did I mention that I am *grounded*?"

"Oh, please," said Zozo. "We've been out here playing together for half an hour. Your parents don't mind."

"That's because they don't know," said Penina. She stood Barb on her hand and had her scan the horizon.

"Then they won't know if you come in for a minute, will they?"

How long could it take to look at an Easter basket? Penina would be back in the yard before anyone knew the difference. Besides, Zozo was trying to be nice and make up for that stupid snowflake stuff.

"One minute?" said Penina.

"Seventy-two seconds, tops," Zozo said.

The Easter basket was a giant wicker laundry hamper. Zozo had painted it lavender and glued on little plastic buttons shaped like roses and tulips. Zozo and her mom were always making each other fabulous, elaborate gifts or going to concerts together or doing each other's hair. Zozo's dad had died when Zozo was a baby, so it was just Zozo and Mrs. Miller in their family.

"Wow. What are you going to put in it?" Penina asked.

"All kinds of stuff I've been collecting—fancy soap, candy, those scented candles from the dollar store. Most of it's in a bag in there." Zozo waved a hand at the closet.

"Can I see?" asked Penina. She couldn't picture it. It would take two of every flavor candle there was to fill that thing. Zozo's house was going to stink.

"Sure. It's the yellow plastic shopping bag. In the back."

Penina went in and rummaged around. She didn't find the shopping bag, but she did find a miniature bridal gown—white, with a big, poofy skirt and a wide, shiny sash.

"Were you in a wedding?" Penina asked.

"No," said Zozo.

"Then why do you have this dress?" Penina brought it out. Even the hanger was fancy. It was wrapped in quilted, satiny cloth and decorated with a little pink bow on the hook.

"That's from my First Communion. Put it back."

Penina had no idea what Zozo was talking about.

"Can I try it on?"

"Oh, yeah, right. Put it back. If my mom finds out we're playing with it, she'll kill me."

Penina doubted that. Zozo could probably put the white gown on Taffy, and Mrs. Miller would just praise Zozo's sense of doggy fashion. Mrs. Miller let Zozo do anything she wanted. In fact, at that very moment, Zozo was plugging in a hot-glue gun and unwinding a spool of purple rickrack around one of the handles on the giant hamper. Penina's parents would never have let her use a glue gun by herself. She'd need safety goggles, asbestos gloves, and parental supervision.

Penina held the gown against her chest. The hem hit between her knees and her ankles. "I won't get it dirty. I'll just try it on and put it right back."

Zozo looked up, but kept her thumb on the rick-rack. "Penina, it's not going to fit you. That's my Communion dress. I got it when I was seven years old."

"Oh." Penina hung it up. She'd known Zozo since they were in preschool, but she'd never seen her in that beautiful gown. Whatever First Communion was, it was dressy.

"Is it like a recital or something?" Penina asked. Zozo had been taking tap and ballet at Miss Shirley's School of Dance for years. Penina thought it sounded like torture—all that stretching and drilling—but she had to admit, the costumes for the dance recitals were pretty nice. Twice a year, Zozo got to dance in something covered in sequins and glitter, with filmy scarves and floaty skirts. The costumes were very dramatic, but this gown wasn't like that.

"No, it's Holy Communion. It's a sacrament."

Penina might have asked what a sacrament was, if Zozo hadn't made it sound like everyone except maybe babies and kindergarteners knew the word.

"I invited you, but you couldn't come," said Zozo.

"Where?"

"To the party for my First Holy Communion. I remember because you missed the party, but you sent a present over anyway. It was a little music box."

"Really? I don't remember that. Can I play it?"

"I don't have it anymore. My cousin Curtis tried to turn the handle the wrong way and ruined it. He promised to buy me a new one, but he never did."

Zozo scowled, and Penina thought cousin Curtis was probably going to get an e-mail re: replacement music box.

Poor Zozo. She'd lost one music box four and a half years ago and was still upset about it. It's a good thing she was an only child. What would she do with a little sister who went through *all* her stuff and ruined *all* her things?

"It was Mimsy's fault," said Penina. She suddenly remembered. "I wanted to go to your party"—even if she didn't exactly understand what it was all about—"but that was the week I spent with my grandparents, when Mimsy was born."

They'd been extra nice to Penina. They bought her ice cream and stacks of coloring books. She should have known something terrible was about to happen.

"Oh, no!" Penina grabbed Barb and squeezed so hard her hand hurt. "I gotta go. What if my mom notices I'm gone? What if Mimsy starts looking for me?"

It had been way more than a minute. Penina

33

didn't even wait for Zozo. She flew down the steps, through the kitchen, into the garage, and out to the yard. She sank down on her side of the campsite and let her heart slow back down to normal. She could feel it beating in her chest, her neck, her hands.

"Hey! Home free," said Zozo, plopping down with Barbara on her side of the camp. "Told you no one would mind."

"She's here! I found her! She's playing with Zozo!" Mimsy shouted.

Penina turned around and saw Mimsy running around the corner of the house. Mom was right behind her.

Mom stopped next to Penina and just missed stepping on Barb. "Zozo," said Mom, "Penina can't play with you today. She is grounded."

Zozo snatched up Barbara and scooted away. "Bye, Penina," she whispered over her shoulder.

Penina tucked Barb under her arm and got slowly to her feet. Mom stood motionless, her hands on her hips. Mimsy, behind her, did the same.

"Congratulations, Penina," said Mom. "You were grounded for one day, but now you're grounded for two. That means no phone, no Internet, no TV or stereo, no DVDs, and no playing with Zozo. Do I make myself clear?"

Mom glared. Mimsy giggled. She tried to disguise

it as a sneeze, but Penina could tell: it was a giggle. Penina looked from Mimsy to Mom and back at Mimsy.

Then she ran as fast as she could across the yard, around the house, and through the front door. She slammed the door behind her, then opened it back up and slammed it again. She tore upstairs and went to her room. She slammed that door, too. Then she sat and stared at the wall.

It was going to be a long couple of days.

6. Don't Give That Away!

"Okay, they're full!" Penina announced.

She stood between a black plastic garbage bag and a brown cardboard carton. The carton once held their new microwave, but now it was overflowing with old toys, books, and clothes. She wasn't grounded anymore, but she still wasn't allowed to call Zozo. She had to finish spring cleaning first.

"Well, let's see." Mom put her hands on her hips and slowly turned her head to look at every part of Penina's room. "A place for everything, and everything in its place." Mom nodded. "Your room looks like the space shuttle."

"Like a formal French garden," Dad added.

"Like one of those campers where everything folds away into the wall, and the kitchen table turns into a bed," said Penina, bouncing on hers.

"I'll take these downstairs," said Dad. He picked up the big trash bag, but when he bent to lift the carton, he said, "Oof! Now that's some heavy *hametz!*"

36

"Dad! It's not *hametz!*" Penina said, smiling. Her dad could be so goofy sometimes. *Hametz* was food: bread, crackers, pretzels, anything that rose in the oven when it was cooked. Every spring, her family cleaned the whole house and got rid of all the leftover *hametz*. It was part of getting ready for Passover. But they didn't just get rid of *hametz*. They vacuumed behind the clothes dryer. They dusted the bookshelves. They sorted their clothes into piles: Dresser, Attic, and Give-away.

"Don't give that away!" said Dad. "I can take it to school." He had opened the heavy carton and pulled out Penina's blue sweater.

"David, it has a big stain, and the buttons are missing," Mom pointed out.

"Doesn't matter," said Dad, feeling a frayed, fuzzy sleeve. Dad was a high-school art teacher. He was always looking for things his students could use in collages and sculptures.

Penina imagined one of Dad's students, a teenager with tattoos and a pierced tongue, using Penina's sweater in a work of art. When she was little, Dad's students had been her babysitters. For a long time, she had thought all babysitters made puppets from your socks and taught you how to dye your hair with Kool-Aid.

These days, when Penina's family went out to the

37

library or the mall, they usually
ran into Dad's former students,
kids in white lipstick or silver
chains, yelling, "Hey, Mr.
Levine, I got accepted to the
Art Institute!" or "I'm really
getting into planographic
printing, Mr. L.!" Sometimes
they added, "Are these your
kids?" And Dad would intro-
duce Penina and Mimsy.

They never met Mom's
students. Even Mom never
met her students. She taught
them online. She had a virtual
classroom of adults who couldn't get to a regular
school. They were sick or lived way out in the country. Some of them were in jail. Mom taught them
math and financial management.

"All right," said Mom. She closed the carton,
overlapping the flaps so they wouldn't fall open.
"Take the whole box. It's not important where it
goes, as long as it goes somewhere. We're leaving the
day after tomorrow, and I want to get this done
before we go."

Mom used her foot to push the box toward

Dad. "Penina, remind me to write a note to Ms. Anderson. She needs to know you're going to miss a few days of school."

Penina quit bouncing. School! She knew her family was going to Grandma and Grandpa's house for the Seder. She knew it took a whole day to get there. She just hadn't put it together to realize that she was going to miss school.

"What if Ms. Anderson won't let me?" she said.

"Will Penina have to stay here?" asked Mimsy. She came in dragging Elgy by his long, striped nightcap. Elgy was a stuffed bear. He was as tall as Mimsy and twice as wide. She had won him in a raffle at the mall. "If Penina stays here, there will be enough room in the car for Elgy," said Mimsy.

"Penina's coming with us," Dad said. He swung the garbage bag over his shoulder and kicked the carton, little by little, toward the door.

Penina felt overwhelmed by the scent of wintergreen gum, even though there wasn't any in the house. She picked Barb up from her pillow and played with her hair. "How many days will I miss?" she asked.

"Just three," said Mom. She sat down next to Penina and tidied her up. She tucked in a tag on Penina's shirt, picked a loose thread off Penina's sleeve, pushed some stray hair off Penina's forehead. "We drive up on Tuesday," she said. "The Seders are Tuesday and Wednesday nights, and we drive back on Thursday."

Three! Three glorious days away from school. Penina hugged Mom. She jumped off the bed and hugged Dad, then Mimsy. Then Elgy.

She would have hugged Daisy, but it was too hard to reach her under the bed. Daisy! What would Daisy do while they were all in Peekskill? They couldn't bring her. She hated the car.

"I have to call Zozo!" Penina shouted, and clattered down the stairs to the Window Phone.

7. A Big, Fat Zero

"Sure, I'll take care of her, but Ms. Anderson is never going to let you go," said Zozo.

It was funny that she sounded so certain, when she looked so wavery. The rain ran down the windows between them, and Penina could hardly see the expression on her friend's face. But she could hear her just fine.

"Never," said Zozo. "She still hasn't gotten over that Easter Bunny letter."

Penina nodded. You could do that on the Window Phone. Zozo was right. Penina had written Alan a short, friendly letter, but Ms. Anderson said it didn't count. She had asked Penina for a letter from the Easter Bunny every day last week. On Friday, Ms. Anderson made Penina watch as she drew a big, fat zero next to Penina's name in the grade book. "It's in pencil," Ms. Anderson had said. "I'll erase it and give you a grade once you complete the assignment."

"So what?" said Penina, not to Ms. Anderson, but to Zozo. "If my parents want me to go to the Seder in Peekskill, what can Ms. Anderson do? Kidnap me?"

It was really raining now. The forsythia bush between the houses was flattened under the downpour, its hundreds of little yellow flowers blown onto the ground.

"No," said Zozo. Now she was nothing but a voice and a blurry shape behind all that water. "She can't kidnap you, but she can flunk you."

Penina groaned. She pressed her cheek against the cold window. She would still be a sixth grader when Zozo was in seventh grade next year. Zozo would have funny Mrs. Northam, or Mr. Mecca, who gave math parties instead of worksheets, but Penina would always have Ms. Anderson.

When Zozo and everyone else in her class went on to seventh grade and eighth grade and high school, Penina would still be in sixth grade. Unless she turned in the Easter Bunny letter. And Penina would never do that.

8. The Worst Thing

Please excuse Penina's absence from school on Tuesday, Wednesday, and Thursday. We will be traveling to be with family for Passover.
Sincerely,
Sonia Levine

The note was in Mom's neat, slanty handwriting, on a pale blue note card with tiny white flowers. Ms. Anderson took a long time to read it.

Penina explained, "It's for the Seder, the special Passover meal."

Ms. Anderson looked up from the note and smiled. "I know what the Seder is," she said. She closed the note card and stuck it in her top desk drawer. "I hope you will enjoy the Seder," she said, "but you're going to miss a lot of school. I'll send your work with you so you can keep up."

"Okay," Penina said. Ms. Anderson was making a big

deal out of nothing. Three days was not a lot of school. How much homework could there possibly be?

By lunchtime, Penina's take-home folder was practically splitting down the back, it was so full. Did Ms. Anderson always give this much homework, or was this especially for Penina? At the big round table in the cafeteria, Penina dropped the folder at her place and plunked her purple lunch bag down on top of it.

"Ew! That is so nasty!" Anne covered her eyes and peeked through her fingers. She was staring at something behind Penina.

Jackie stood up and looked where Anne was looking. "Ugh! Repulsive." She squeezed her eyes shut and dropped back into her chair.

Zozo turned around to see, and Penina did the same. She saw Ryan's orange head. That wasn't nasty. But then she saw what was grossing out Jackie and Anne. Jesse and Timmy were making a pile of food. They'd heaped tater tots on top of meatloaf and stacked Jell-O jewels on top of that. They'd poured chocolate milk over the whole thing, and now they were sprinkling it with green peas.

Timmy grinned at Zozo. "Want a taste?"

"That's the worst thing I've ever seen," Penina murmured.

44

"I've seen worse," said Zozo. Penina had been talking to Zozo, but Zozo was talking to the boys. "That's wasteful, but it's not really bad. I bet I've seen the worst thing of anyone here."

"Yeah?" said Jesse. "What'd you see?"

"I'm not telling you," Zozo said.

The boys groaned.

"Yet," Zozo added. "It's a bet. I'll tell you once you ante up."

Zozo was always saying things like "ante up" and "who's in?" Her mom played cards with a bunch of ladies from work, so Zozo knew the lingo.

She reached into her bag and took out a millet muffin. It was as big as a softball and covered with crunchy apple topping. Her allergies kept her from eating most kinds of desserts, so her mom made her these muffins. They were famous.

"Oh," said the boys, all together.

Zozo placed the muffin on a napkin in the middle of the big round table. "Who's in?"

"Me," said Timmy. He threw a candy bar down in front of Penina. "This one time, my dog—"

"Hold on," Zozo interrupted him. "You have to wait till everyone antes up. Ryan, you in?"

"I don't know," said Ryan. He didn't exactly blush, but his neck got pinker.

"Aw, come on," said Jesse.

"Yeah. You got nachos. You have to bet those," said Timmy.

"No, he doesn't," said Zozo. "Ryan, you be the judge. Who else is in? Penina?"

Penina looked inside her purple lunch bag. She knew what she had; she'd packed it herself: a cheese

sandwich with mustard, an orange, carrot and celery sticks, and half a dozen soft mini chocolate-chip cookies, the last of the *hametz* in the house. They were from the supermarket, not homemade like Zozo's muffin, but they'd get her into the game.

She put them beside Timmy's candy bar and Zozo's muffin. "I'm in," she declared. She wished she had a

hat. A gambler should always wear a lucky hat, something with a brim. She was pretty sure she once had a Pittsburgh Pirates cap. It had a place in the back for her to put her ponytail through. She hadn't seen it in a while. She'd have to check Mimsy's room. Mimsy had probably taken it when she took the henin.

Something bounced onto the table and rolled across to Penina. A round pink snack cake, covered in coconut shavings and wrapped in plastic.

"I'm in," yelled Jesse.

"Good," said Zozo, "anyone else? Anne? Jackie?"

"Ok," said Anne. She slid a bag of potato chips into the middle.

"I don't think so," said Jackie. "I'll co-judge." She smiled at Ryan. He nodded.

"Do we have to look at that barferocious tower the whole time?" said Anne.

No one wanted to do that, so they made room for the boys at their table. Penina ended up between Timmy and Zozo, with Ryan across from her.

Zozo laid out the rules. "It has to be something you've really seen, not something you saw on TV, and not something someone told you about, okay?"

Everyone nodded.

"And the judges' decision is final."

"What if the judges disagree?" Penina asked.

Zozo looked impatient.

"We'll do rock, paper, scissors," said Ryan.

Timmy was first. "The worst thing I ever saw was when my dog had a tapeworm."

Penina pressed her lips together. This was going to be gross.

"The vet squeezed her butt and all this brown water gushed out. You could see the worms in it. They looked like wiggly white grains of rice. Definitely the worst thing I've ever seen."

He grinned at Ryan and Jackie, then leaned back in his chair with his fingers laced behind his head. Penina tried not to picture the tapeworms in a smelly brown puddle. She tried to imagine something nice. Lemonade. Pink dogwood blossoms. The Sacagawea dollar.

"Anne?" said Jackie. She was taking notes. She'd written *Timmy—dog's butt* on the back of an old spelling test.

"Well, I saw a squirrel get run over by a garbage truck. It made a popping sound underneath the truck's tires. One second it was gray and fluffy and scampering across the street. The next it was just a flat, red smear." She shook her head. Penina could tell Anne was still seeing that squirrel, over and over in her head.

She watched Jackie write *Anne—popped squirrel.*

"Now me," said Jesse. "My dad once sliced his hand open. He was trying to cut a grapefruit, but I guess he was holding it the wrong way. The blood soaked through two kitchen towels. He has this knobby white Frankenstein-looking scar now, all across here." Jesse drew an imaginary line from his pointer finger to the pinky side of his wrist.

Penina traced a line across her hand. How would it feel to have a cut that big? Jesse's father must have cried.

"That's nothing," said Zozo. You know those concrete steps in front of the post office? I once saw a kid fall off his skateboard onto those steps. He scraped the skin off half his face. He didn't even try to stop the blood or anything. He just sat there howling, with blood dripping down his neck and shirt."

"What did you do?" Penina asked. Zozo had never told her about this before.

"Nothing. My mom and I were across the street. A lady ran out from that big gray church next door. She was yelling at him for skating on the steps, but she was giving him her scarf and calling 911 at the same time."

"So he was okay?" asked Jackie, pen poised for note taking.

"Well, not at first," said Zozo. "I mean, the guy

50

skinned half his face off—eyebrow and everything. It was the worst, worst thing I've ever seen."

Penina wished she'd never gotten into this contest. Now she'd have these pictures in her head forever: bloody hands and faces, squirrels under tires, squirming parasites.

"Penina? You ready?" Ryan asked.

Penina looked at the pile of treats, not that she had any appetite left for any of it. But it would be cool to win. What was the worst thing she had ever seen?

A kitty-litter box full of ammonia-smelling chunks?

A booger stuck to the pencil sharpener on Ms. Anderson's desk?

A glass of milk with clotted, clumpy lumps at the bottom?

Thinking about it made Penina's jaws clench. Her stomach wanted to crawl up and out and run away forever. It was the same way she'd felt—

"At the Schaeffer Park playground. You know that climber they have that's all tunnels?"

"Uh-huh," Zozo said. Jackie and Anne nodded.

"Mimsy, my sister, climbed up in there last summer and wouldn't come out."

Zozo made a sound like *tsk*. She'd heard this story before. Was she anticipating victory? Or acknowledging defeat?

Penina continued, "My mom was freaking out.

51

She stood there at the end of the tunnel, screaming, 'Mimsy! Come out! Come to Mommy!'"

Anne and Timmy laughed.

Penina frowned. This was supposed to be awful, not funny. "Mimsy didn't say anything, but we could hear her whimpering and snuffling. Mom tried to climb in, but she couldn't fit."

Mom wasn't exactly fat. She just had kind of a big bottom. Those tunnels weren't very wide.

"So I crawled up to get her, and I saw why she wasn't coming out."

Penina swallowed hard. Her lunch, her breakfast, and last night's dinner all wanted to come back up.

"She was huddled up in the joint between two tubes. In front of her, with his arms spread out to block the whole tunnel, was a big, ugly boy."

Not that big, really. He was probably seven or eight, but bigger than Mimsy.

"'Leave her alone!' I shouted.

"I moved over so he could get past me, but he went out the other way, past Mimsy. As he went by Mimsy, he pinched her leg and—"

Penina didn't even want to tell this part, but she'd already gotten this far. Besides, this was a bet.

"And spat at her. She got a big yellow hawker on her chest."

Penina pressed her hand against her mouth. Hard. *Don't think about it. Picture daffodils. Chocolate brownies. Your best blue gel pen.*

"A hawker? That's it? No blood? No worms? Big deal," said Timmy. He was already reaching for Anne's bag of potato chips.

Ryan pulled it away and tossed it back onto the pile. "So? All you've got is a dog's butt," he said. "What makes you think you're the winner?"

Ryan and Jackie went to the boys' table to whisper and go over their notes. Penina cupped her chin in her hand and tried to hear what they were saying. She peeked sideways at Zozo. Zozo smiled and raised her eyebrows, like *Well, we'll see.*

9. Judges' Decisions Are Final

Ryan and Jackie came back and sat down. No one said a word. Jackie and Ryan looked at each other, looked at the prizes, and pushed them across the table till they were all squarely in front of Penina.

"Congrats," said Ryan.

"You win," said Jackie.

"No fair!" said Timmy.

"No way a hawker is grosser than my dad's cut hand," Jesse added.

"Judges' decisions are final," said Zozo. "Congratulations, Penina." She gave Penina a pat on the back, kind of a hard pat, but still friendly.

Anne nodded. "Penina saw the grossest thing, that's all."

"Not really," said Jackie.

"The contest wasn't who saw the grossest thing," said Ryan. "It was who saw the worst thing."

"Same difference," said Jesse.

54

Ryan frowned at Jesse like, *Are you a moron?*

"Picking on a little kid, that's the worst," Ryan said.

"Yeah, doggy worms don't even come close," said Jackie.

"Thanks, Jackie. Thanks, Ryan," Penina said.

Ryan shrugged. He went back to his table with Jesse and Timmy.

"Here," Penina offered, "let's divide this up."

"No, thanks," said Anne, "I'm not exactly hungry right now."

Jackie made pushing-away motions. "No, it's yours. You won it yourself," she said.

"You keep it. I can't eat most of that stuff anyway," Zozo said.

"You can eat the muffin," said Penina.

They split the muffin four ways, and they had just enough time to finish before the bell rang for class.

Penina was the last one back from lunch. She had to stash her winnings in her locker, and it took a while because the pink coconut snack cake kept rolling out. She finally decided she might as well eat it, but it was stale, and she had to go against the flow of hallway traffic to get back to the "Don't Be a Litterbug" barrel by the cafeteria doors.

By the time the second bell rang, she'd made it back to her classroom, but not back to her seat. Her desk was the fourth one in the third row. She had to squeeze past everyone else already at their desks.

"Chhhaak!" Jesse made a throat-clearing sound, the kind of sound a person makes to bring up a glob of mucus.

Penina was standing beside him when he did it, and her mind filled with the picture of that brat in the tunnel spitting on her little sister. Her stomach rolled, tightened, and sent a stream of recently ingested lunch up Penina's throat and out onto Jesse. Onto Jesse's desk. Onto Jesse's Language Arts book. Onto Jesse's fat four-color ballpoint pen.

"Hey!" yelled Jesse. He flicked the vomit off his hands and his pen.

"Hey!" yelled Penina. He didn't have to fling it onto her. It was his own fault she'd thrown up on him. She jumped back and checked her clothes for spatters. All clear. But she had to wash her face, had to rinse her mouth, maybe get some paper towels for Jesse.

"I'll be right back!" she yelled to Ms. Anderson.

Ms. Anderson waved at Penina but didn't say anything, or if she did say something, Penina didn't know what it was. It was hard to understand what Ms. Anderson was saying. She was covering her mouth as if she was trying not to laugh.

10. Soda Crackers and Ginger Ale

Penina had always thought it was a rumor, but it turned out there was an actual rule that if you threw up at school, you were sent home for the day.

"Just sit tight, hon." Mrs. Mulrane, the school secretary, pointed at a row of chairs lined up by the principal's door: orange, yellow, green, blue. Penina sat in the green one. These chairs were where the bad kids sat when they were sent to Dr. Tobin's office. If anyone came by while she was waiting, they'd think she had gotten into trouble. Penina narrowed her eyes. She stuck out her bottom teeth. She crossed her arms. That's how the bad kids sat.

"Penina, are you okay? You're not going to get sick again, are you?" Dr. Tobin had a very deep voice, like a bass drum. It could startle you if you weren't ready for it.

Penina opened her eyes, closed her mouth, and

put her hands beside her on the green seat. "No, I'm fine," she said. She hadn't seen him come out of his office.

"I just got off the phone with your dad," Dr. Tobin said. He was very tall, so tall Penina thought his head would scrape the ceiling if he stood up all the way. It's a good thing he was bald. Having hair might have made him too tall to fit through the doorway.

"He asked me to tell you he's on his way."

"Okay," Penina said.

Dr. Tobin checked his watch. He held his hands together behind him and rocked back on his heels. He let go of his hands and pushed his glasses up his nose. "Bit of a bug going around?" he said.

Penina nodded. Jesse was a bit of a bug.

"When I was your age, if I had an upset stomach, my mother gave me soda crackers and ginger ale," Dr. Tobin announced. From the look on his face, Penina guessed soda crackers and ginger ale were his favorite foods in the whole entire world.

"You tell your dad I said to give you soda crackers and ginger ale—as much as you want." He smiled, and Penina could see that his four front top teeth were whiter than the others.

"Penina!" said Dad. He strode across the room to her. First he tugged her braid; then he felt her forehead.

58

"Hi, Dad. I don't have a fever," she said.

Dad let go of Penina and shook hands with Dr. Tobin.

"You got here fast, Dave."

"I came as quickly as I could," Dad said. "Thank you for looking after Penina." He gave Penina's other braid a tug.

"Don't mention it. We had a nice talk. I was just telling her my mother's cure for the stomachache: soda crackers and ginger ale."

"Yeah, my mom gave us that, too," said Dad.

59

Crackers and ginger ale must be some wonder drug, the way these two talked about it. There weren't any soda crackers at Penina's house. She knew that for a fact. She'd thrown away an almost-empty box as part of the great *hametz* roundup.

Dad picked up Penina's jacket, her lunch bag, and her overstuffed backpack. He carried it all to the car. Penina didn't have to hold anything but Dad's big, square hand.

"Are you going to be all right to go to Grandma and Grandpa's tomorrow?" Dad asked on the drive home.

Of course she was. She wasn't even sick. She explained the whole thing, from the mushed-up food tower to Dr. Tobin's mother's stomachache remedy.

"Congratulations," said Dad. "Where's the loot?"

Penina didn't know. She tried to remember what had happened to it. When she came back to the classroom, Mr. Cooke had been there with a cartload of equipment: brooms, dustpans, buckets, mops, towels, bags, brushes, and a big box of sand that looked like kitty litter and smelled like cherry cough drops. He had sprinkled it all over the mess and whisked the whole mixture into a black plastic bag.

"Sorry, Mr. Cooke," Penina had whispered.

"That's okay," Mr. Cooke had answered, "I've seen

worse." It was a good thing Mr. Cooke hadn't been in the contest. He would have won for sure.

After that, it had been a confusion of worksheets and assignments and being hustled down the hall to Mrs. Mulrane. Penina had no idea what had happened to her winnings.

"They might be in my locker," she said.

"That's too bad," said Dad. "But look at it this way: better to leave it at school than to take it home. It's all *hametz*."

It was, but was having it in her school locker any better than having it at home? "Doesn't it still count as my *hametz*?" she said.

"That's a good question, Penina." Dad smiled in his teacherly way. "Does the contents of your locker belong to you or to the school? This is a matter for discussion and interpretation. Remember to ask Grandpa when you see him tomorrow."

Grandpa loved that kind of thing. Penina would be sure to ask. That is, if she could ever get a word in around Mimsy's talk talk talk talk talk.

11. 217 Minutes

Four more hours. That was 240 minutes. That was the time it took to watch eight television shows. That was how long it would be before they got to Grandma and Grandpa's house, and they'd already been on the road for two hours. It was almost 8:30.

One hundred miles behind them, Zozo was climbing the steps to the school, putting her jacket and lunch bag in her locker, taking her seat and smiling at Ms. Anderson. Penina hoped Zozo would remember to get the *hametz* out of her locker. Penina had explained the whole thing to her on the Window Phone last night, and Zozo said she'd take care of it.

Penina crossed her legs and kicked the back of the driver's seat.

"Watch the feet, Penina," said her dad. "I need to concentrate on the driving here." To Mom, he added, "Are you sure you didn't see a sign for Route 80?"

"I don't think so. All this construction makes it hard to be sure," Mom said, and added, "Penina, try to relax. You won't make the trip any shorter by fidgeting. Why don't you try to go to sleep, like Mimsy?"

Mimsy smiled in her "sleep" and snuggled into her booster seat.

"She's awake, Mom," Penina reported.

"Shh, don't wake her," Mom whispered.

"How can I wake her when she's already awake?" Penina said.

Mimsy squinched her eyes shut and made a fake-o snoring sound, *"Hah-shhhh, hah-shhhh."*

"Hey, Sleeping Beauty," said Dad.

"She wasn't sleeping," Penina muttered, "and she's definitely not a beauty," she added, even more softly. Penina whooshed the pages of *The Westing Game*. It was a good book, and she'd *almost* figured out the solution to the mystery before Turtle did. But she'd started reading it two days ago and finished it fifteen minutes into the trip, so now she didn't have anything to read.

Before she even noticed what was happening, her foot was tapping at the back of Dad's seat.

"Penina!" Mom and Dad shouted at once.

"I can't help it. It's so boring here. Zozo Miller has a DVD player in her car," Penina observed.

"Well, we're not the Millers," Mom answered. "In the Levine family, car time is family time. Let's have a sing-along!"

"I want to sing the bicycle song!" yelled Mimsy.

Penina didn't object. If they had to have a sing-along, which they evidently did, and if Mimsy got to pick the songs, which of course she did (why should this trip be different than any other trip?), then "Bicycle Built for Two" was probably the least painful way to do it.

"Daisy, Daisy," sang Mom. Mimsy and Penina joined in halfway through the second "Daisy." Penina didn't mind this song. She imagined she was singing it to her cat, Daisy. For the second verse, the one where Daisy answers, she replaced some of the words with "meow." She sounded like Henrietta Pussycat from Mister Rogers' Neighborhood of Make-Believe.

Mimsy thought that was hilarious, and she made them sing the meow verse over and over until Dad asked them what was next on the program.

"Penina, why don't you pick," said Mom.

"Can we sing *'Eliyahu'*?" Penina asked. If they were on their way to the Seder, they might as well sing Passover songs. *"Eliyahu"* was her favorite one. The other Passover songs were kind of jokey and jolly. *"Eliyahu"* was slow and elegant. Her grandma, mom, and aunts had this really pretty way of harmonizing at the end. The song was in Hebrew, so Penina had no idea what it meant, but it was probably the most beautiful song she knew.

"Sure," said Mom. "It'll be a warm-up for tonight."

"Eliyahu ha-navi," they sang. Dad joined in, and Mimsy did, too, even though she didn't know all the words.

"Eliyahu ha-tishbe

"Eliyahu, Eliyahu

"Eli-ya-ah-hu ha-gil-a-di."

They naturally harmonized on the last lines, and Penina took the high part.

It sounded so pretty, the way their voices blended together over the sound of the motor and the wind rushing past the car.

"David! Where are you going? Didn't you see the exit?" The song stopped abruptly as Mom shouted and grabbed Dad's arm.

"No! All I saw was about a thousand orange cones!" yelled Dad. "Why didn't you tell me the exit was coming?"

"I was singing with the girls!" said Mom.

"Well, so was I!" said Dad.

For a while, no one said anything else. Penina looked out the window at the cows and the trees and the orange cones lined up forever along the side of the highway.

Finally, the car stopped and Dad opened the window. A man with a ponytail and a plastic orange vest strolled up to the car.

"Excuse me," Dad said to the man, "but can you tell me how to get back to Route 80? We missed our exit."

The man looked past Dad and smiled at Penina and Mimsy. "Hello, ladies," he said, tipping his hard hat. "Out for a drive?"

"We're going to Grandma's house!" Mimsy shouted.

"Oh, really?" said the man, smiling even bigger now. "Well, you be sure to stick to the path and don't take any shortcuts through the woods, now, okay?"

What was he talking about?

"Mom, what's he talking about?" Penina whispered, but the man heard, too.

"The young lady looks like Little Red Riding Hood in that sweatshirt of hers," he explained.

Mimsy bounced in her booster. She did look a little like Red Riding Hood, if Red Riding Hood wore a ten-sizes-too-big hoodie handed down from one of her father's art students.

"You got a map?" asked the man.

Dad got out the map, and the man got out a pen and showed them how to get to Grandma and Grandpa's.

They got there in 217 minutes.

12. Ugly Children

"I get to ring the doorbell, and I get the bed by the wall, and I get to sit next to Grandma at the Seder!" yelled Mimsy. She was halfway up the front lawn by the time she finished saying it, but Penina could hear every word because Mimsy had left the car door open.

Penina unbuckled her seat belt and climbed out of the car. She picked up her book and Barb before shutting her door and going around to close Mimsy's. It wasn't fair. Mimsy always got to ring the doorbell.

Grandma and Grandpa's whole front yard was the side of a big hill. At the top, Grandma was already hugging Mimsy. Penina trudged up the path slower and slower until she stopped. An hour ago, she couldn't wait to get to Grandma and Grandpa's house. Now, all she wanted to do was get back in the car and go home. What was the big deal about the Seder anyway? She didn't like gefilte fish, she couldn't stand hard-boiled eggs, and she didn't know how to read Hebrew.

"Come on, Penina, Grandma's waiting," said Mom. She guided Penina up the hill with her fingertips on Penina's back.

Grandma threw her arms open when she saw Mom and Penina. "Oh! Another ugly granddaughter!" she said. "Sonia, your kids get uglier every time I see them!" Grandma squeezed Penina close and gave her a loud smooch on the cheek. "Uh-oh. I got lipstick on your face. Come here, darling." Grandma rubbed away her mouth-print. "Have you ever seen such ugly children?"

Penina smiled. She was about 98 percent sure Grandma was kidding.

Penina followed Grandma and Mimsy into the kitchen. A tall silver pot boiled and bubbled on the stove. Heaps of parsley and celery towered over the cutting board. The oven light was on, and Penina could see a crackly brown potato kugel baking inside. She took a deep breath. *Ahh.*

"Can I have a macaroon?" asked Mimsy. "Did you get egg matzah or just the regular kind? I only like egg, and I *don't* like *maror!*"

Penina had to agree with Mimsy this time. *Maror*—the grated horseradish root they ate at the

Seder—stung her eyes and made her nose run. She didn't know how anyone could stand it.

"Chocolate!" said Mimsy, reaching for a canister of double-fudge macaroons. "Can you open this?"

"Oh, my poor, starving grandchildren," said Grandma. She opened the canister and gave it back to Mimsy. "Here you go, sweet-cheeks."

Mimsy took it to a corner and sat down. She put

two macaroons in her mouth at once. They weren't that big, but still. Penina didn't think *she* could do that.

"Wow," she said. "How many can you fit in at a time?"

Mimsy held up ten fingers, but Penina never got to see for herself. Dad came in and found her counting out a line of macaroons.

"That's enough, girls. You'll ruin your dinner. Penina, go help Grandma. Mimsy, why don't you see if you can unpack with Mommy. I'll take the macaroons."

Mimsy jumped up and ran toward the bedroom. "I get the blue hangers!" she shouted.

Dad took the macaroons into the den, and Penina found Grandma standing at the sink, running water over a colander of hard-boiled eggs.

"You know the drill, Penina," Grandma said. "I find you in my kitchen, I put you to work."

"I know," Penina said.

"Peel these, please." Grandma hoisted the eggs onto the counter and plunked down a big ceramic bowl. It was white, with little pink rosebuds painted around the rim. "Thatta girl," she said. She gave Penina's arm a quick squeeze.

Nothing could make Penina eat a hard-boiled egg, but she liked peeling them. She took a warm egg and pressed it against the counter. The shell gave a satisfying crunch, and Penina watched the net of cracks grow as she rolled the egg beneath her palm. The trick was to loosen up the shell without breaking the white part underneath. Perfect. The egg was slick and smooth and kind of rubbery. Penina placed it in the rosebud bowl and threw the shells in the sink.

Penina rolled and peeled: four eggs, five, six.

"Do you know why we have eggs at the Seder?" said Grandma.

"Uh-huh," Penina said. Mrs. Greenbaum had been over it with them a hundred times in religious school. "It's to remind us of springtime and the rebirth of nature and all that."

"Sure," said Grandma. "But there's more to it than that. Other foods get soft when you cook them. Potatoes, beans, cheese, fish—the hotter the oven, the softer they get. Not eggs. An egg, when you cook it, gets hard." She took an egg from the colander and tapped it on the counter. "That's like the Jewish people," she said. "When the heat is on, we don't turn to mush. We get tougher."

"Like when we were slaves in Egypt," said Penina.

"That's right."

"And when Haman wanted to kill us."

"Yes," said Grandma, "like that."

"And when all those Jews came over from Russia," said Penina.

Grandma nodded. Her grandfather had come to America when he was seventeen. The Russian tsar had made life very hard for the Jews in his country. Thousands escaped to America. Thousands more had died.

"And, it's like when Ms. Anderson tried to make me write a letter as the Easter Bunny."

Grandma put down her egg and stared at Penina. "She what?"

Penina told Grandma the whole story.

Grandma hugged Penina hard. "Oh, my little hard-boiled egg," she said. "You make your grandmother so proud."

Penina smiled. She was 100 percent sure Grandma meant it.

13. The Tricky Thing about Horseradish

Penina didn't know much Hebrew. But she could say the blessing over matzah along with everyone else: *"al akheelat matzah."*

She bit into her piece of matzah, and matzah crumbs sprinkled down across her plate, the tablecloth, and the front of her fancy green dress. It tasted all right, like a thick saltine cracker without the salt.

"My grandfather, the rabbi, always led the Seder in Hebrew," said Grandpa. He was at the head of the table, way over in the dining room. Penina's end of the table was in the living room. There were so many uncles, aunts, cousins, and neighbors at the Seder, they filled two long tables. Penina leaned forward to see Grandpa.

"Because Hebrew is the language of prayer," said Grandpa. He told this story every year. "But he realized that not everyone knew Hebrew, so he always gave each section again, in Yiddish, which is what

74

his family spoke at home. Of course, this was the twentieth century; his family had come to a new country, and now they might have guests who didn't speak Yiddish, so he was careful to tell the story again. In Polish. Then in German. I was fifteen years old before I ever heard the Seder in a language I could understand."

"That was at my house," said Grandma. She rested her hand on Grandpa's arm. "My family had our own way of conducting the Seder. We read one page of the Haggadah, then we ate and sang labor songs for four hours."

"That's right," said Grandpa. "I still think 'Bread and Roses' is a Passover song."

"That would be *unleavened* 'Bread and Roses,' Grandpa," Naomi said.

The grown-ups cracked up. Penina grinned. Unleavened bread was another name for matzah.

"Pretty good, Naomi," Penina said. She hoped Naomi could visit her in Pennsylvania some time. Zozo would love her.

"Naomi," said Grandpa, "would you please ask the Four Questions?"

Naomi didn't reach for her Haggadah. Penina squeezed her hand under the table. Maybe Naomi was scared to read aloud in front of all these people. But Naomi didn't seem scared. She looked up the long table at Grandpa and Grandma and sang, *"Mah Nishtanah ha-lyla ha-zeh."*

She had them memorized. In Hebrew. Penina felt like clapping, but you didn't clap for people who read at the Seder. It wasn't polite.

Penina smiled at Naomi, and when Grandpa said it was time, she made Naomi a Hillel sandwich.

"Here, I'll make it so it won't burn your eyelashes off," Penina said. She took two pieces of matzah and covered them with sweet, sticky, crunchy *haroset*. She

patted the mixture of apples, walnuts, cinnamon, and honey down with the flat side of her knife, as if she were spreading mortar on bricks. Her great-great-great-—more greats than she could count—great-grandparents had used mortar to build brick walls for Pharaoh under the blazing hot sun, when they were slaves in Egypt.

Life under slavery was bitter, bitter as the strongest horseradish in the world. The tricky thing about horseradish was that it looked so harmless. If you just

saw it and didn't breathe in, you might think it was shredded coconut, but if you inhaled anywhere near it, you knew it wasn't sweet. (Actually, it was a shredded root. Penina had watched Grandma run the gray, twisted thing along the grater. There was also the red kind of horseradish that came in a jar. It wasn't quite as hot, but it was nowhere to be seen on this Seder table.) Just the smell of the grated horseradish made Penina's eyes water and her throat burn. She felt like holding her nose and passing the bowl back up the table.

But without horseradish, it wouldn't be a Hillel sandwich, and without the Hillel sandwich, the Seder wouldn't be the same. Penina took the horseradish spoon and scooped exactly three shreds of horseradish onto Naomi's haroset. She did the same to hers, and covered each one with another piece of matzah.

"Here you go," she said to Naomi. They counted to three and bit into their Hillel sandwiches together.

"Go!" yelled Mimsy. Mimsy was sitting next to Grandma, one room and two long tables away, but Penina could still hear her shouting and giggling. Everyone could. "Go wash your hands, Grandpa. Hurry."

Grandpa stood up and pushed in his chair. "Well, yes, now that you mention it, Mimsy, I guess my hands are a little dirty. Why don't I go upstairs and wash up?"

"Okay!" Mimsy squealed, pulling Grandpa toward the doorway. Penina didn't squeal, but she and Naomi grinned at each other, and her feet started drumming against her chair legs: *tapita tapita tapita.*

"Now, while I'm upstairs, I don't want anyone touching the *Afikoman,*" said Grandpa. He scrunched down his eyebrows to look stern, but he was smiling as much as Penina and Naomi. "The *Afikoman* is very important. We can't finish the Seder without it."

"All right already. Wash your hands," said Grandma. She pushed Grandpa in a gentle way, and he left the dining room.

"I got it!" yelled Mimsy. Penina's grin collapsed. Of course Mimsy got there first. She was a mile and a half closer to the head of the table than Penina was. Mimsy held up the package she had grabbed off the table. It was a napkin wrapped around a piece of matzah, a special matzah: the *Afikoman.*

It could be worth a lot.

14. The Afikoman

Naomi jumped up and ran to Grandpa's empty seat.
Penina followed her. So did the neighbors' kids and
the cousins from Long Island Penina saw only once
a year. They crowded around Penina's little sister,
who was hugging the *Afikoman* to her chest.

"Give me the *Afikoman*, Mimsy," said Naomi, "I
know just where to hide it."

Mimsy squinted at Naomi for a long moment,
and Penina wondered if she would have to knock
Mimsy down and wrench the *Afikoman* out of her
arms, but then Mimsy passed the bundle over to
Naomi, and Penina relaxed.

Grandma and Grandpa had an old-fashioned stereo
they called the hi-fi. It couldn't play tapes or CDs, but
it had a big spinner for their old record albums. Naomi
lifted the lid and put the *Afikoman* right on the spinner.

"Ah," sighed Penina. Grandpa would never find
the *Afikoman* there.

"I hope no one is touching the *Afikoman*!" yelled

Grandpa. Penina heard him coming down the stairs. "I'm coming back. I'm finished washing my hands."

"Sit down! Quickly," squeaked Penina. She was trying to shout and whisper at the same time. Naomi and Mimsy and the neighbors and the cousins all scrambled for their chairs. Penina sat down, put her napkin on her lap, and folded her hands just as Grandpa stepped back into the room.

"Why, Irving," said Grandma, "what clean hands you have."

"All the better to serve you with, my dear," said Grandpa. And he poured Grandma a glass of wine.

Penina poured grape juice for herself and Naomi. Kids were allowed to drink some wine at the Seder, but Penina stuck with grape juice. Even a little wine gave her a headache, and it tasted like rotten fruit, gross.

There was an awful lot of gross food to get through before the Seder got good. First came hard-boiled eggs, like giant naked eyeballs. Next was gefilte fish, which always made Penina want to sing, "Great gray gobs of gushy gross gefilte fish" to the tune of "Greasy Grimy Gopher Guts."

Penina drank her juice and waited to be served something edible.

"How many matzah balls do you want, Penina?" Mom called down the table.

"None," Penina said.

Mom shook her head. "You're missing the best part," she said, but she passed down a bowl of matzah ball soup the way Penina liked it: matzah-ball-free. Penina held her spoon the fancy way, sipping broth from the side. Mmm. It was chicken soup, clear gold with specks of parsley and carrot, perfect the way it was. Penina thought it was crazy to go messing it up with lumpy matzah-meal dumplings.

The soup was good, but it got better after that. Penina passed platter after platter. She took beef, chicken, potato kugel, cole slaw, black olives, and an extra-large helping of carrot ring. Around the table, the grown-ups groaned.

"Oh, I'm so full. Everything was so good."

"Trudy, I look forward to your potato kugel every Passover."

"I ate too much. I'll never have room for the *Afikoman*."

Naomi and Penina looked at each other and covered their grins with their napkins. Penina leaned in and looked up the table for Mimsy. The mention of *Afikoman* was probably sending her into a frenzy. But Mimsy wasn't there. The seat next to Grandma was empty. No, Penina saw, it was *almost* empty. Mimsy had slid down so far in her seat, only a few wild brown curls could be seen above the table. Penina

82

ducked under the table to get a better look. Mimsy's head was resting on the arm of Grandma's chair. Her cheeks were red, and she was fast asleep.

Penina tugged on Naomi's dress. "Come here," she said, "look."

Naomi bent down and looked at Mimsy. "She had too much wine," Naomi said.

"Girls, come back. Where are you going?"

Penina and Naomi sat up. Mom was holding a tray of macaroons and waiting for an answer.

"We were just checking on Mimsy," said Penina.

Mom put down the tray and turned toward Mimsy. "Oh dear," said Mom, "my baby has passed out."

Grandma patted Mimsy's head. "Don't worry, Sonia," she said, "she's not drunk, just tired. It's been a big day."

Daddy stood up and lifted Mimsy out of her chair. She didn't even open her eyes. She just put her

83

head on Daddy's shoulder and kept on sleeping as Daddy carried her away.

Then came the macaroons. And gummi-candy fruit slices, and chocolate almond bark, and sponge cake with strawberry topping.

Penina leaned back in her chair. It was hard work, eating such a big meal.

Grandpa said a prayer in Hebrew, and the grown-ups mumbled, *"Aw-main,"* amen in Hebrew. Around the tables, people started picking up their Haggadahs, flipping through the pages to where they'd left off before the meal.

Penina reached behind her. She had stashed her Haggadah against the back of her chair so it wouldn't get food on it. It wasn't there.

"It's gone!" said Grandpa. "I can't find it!" He held his hands out in front of him, as if he were showing how empty they were. "We can't finish the Seder without it. What are we going to do?"

It took Penina a minute to realize Grandpa was not talking about her Haggadah. She squeezed Naomi's hand. Naomi squeezed back.

"Maybe the children know where it is," said Grandma. "Why don't you ask them, Irving?"

"Of course," said Grandpa, "the children will help me. Children, do you know where to find the *Afikoman*?"

"Yes!" they yelled. Even without Mimsy, they were loud enough to shake the glasses on the table.

"Very good," Grandpa said. "Children, bring me the *Afikoman*, and then we can go on with the Seder."

Penina and Naomi and the cousins and the neighbors squirmed in their chairs. They grinned at one another. They looked at Grandpa and shook their heads.

"No?" Grandpa put his hand on his chest, shocked. "You have the *Afikoman* and yet you refuse to give it to your grandfather? Your host?"

Grandpa looked like he really wanted the *Afikoman*.

"Naomi," said Grandpa, "you're a good girl. I know *you* will get the *Afikoman* for your old grandpa, won't you?"

The grown-ups chuckled and rolled their eyes, but Naomi stood up and demanded, "What will you give us for it?"

"Yeah!" shouted the cousins and the neighbors. The grownups laughed. Penina put her arm around Naomi's shoulders. "Way to go!" said Penina.

"What?" said Grandpa. "Am I being squeezed by my own flesh and blood?"

Grandma beamed at Grandpa. "I'm afraid so, honey. What are you going to give them?"

15. Thumbs Down

"What can I give them but my thanks and a satisfactory conclusion to our Passover Seder?" Grandpa said.

"Boo!" said the kids. They made the thumbs-down sign all around the tables.

"You'll have to do better than that," Grandma told Grandpa. "What else you got?"

"Well, I might have something in the den," Grandpa said. "I'll see."

The den was right next to the dining room, so Grandpa was gone for only one second. When he came back, he had a big, shiny purple gift bag.

One bag. Eight children. Nine, if you counted Mimsy. Maybe the bag was just for Naomi. She was the one who actually hid the *Afikoman*. Penina couldn't take her eyes off the bag. She saw Grandpa reach in and pull out . . .

A wide, flat rectangle wrapped in pale blue paper. "Geoffrey," he said. One of the Long Island cousins stood up. Grandpa passed him the gift.

"Naomi," said Grandpa. "Penina."

Two identical blue rectangles made their way down the table. Naomi kept one and passed the other to Penina. Almost identical. Naomi's was sealed with a glossy yellow chick-shaped sticker. The chick had NAOMI written across its tummy in square capital letters. Grandma must have wrapped the gifts. Her notes all looked like she was SHOUTING, but it was just how she wrote. Penina knew the story.

"You know why Grandma only uses all caps?" she whispered to Naomi.

"No, why?"

"She's left-handed. When she was little, you weren't allowed to write with your left hand."

Naomi interrupted, "What do you mean, weren't allowed?"

Penina nodded. That part hadn't made sense to her, either, the first time she had heard the story. Penina explained it to Naomi just the way Grandma had explained it to her: matter-of-factly. Her voice said, *This is the way it was. The truth may be unpleasant, but I'm not going to lie to you.* "They told her to write with her right hand. If they saw her holding a pencil in her left hand, they took it away. She was supposed to sit on her left hand to keep from using it."

Penina stuck her right hand under her leg and picked up her juice glass with her left. (She was

87

right-handed, so she had to do the sit-on-your-hand thing in reverse.) She managed to take a sip without spilling any, but it wasn't easy.

Naomi tucked her right hand underneath her and did the same. "That's hard," she said. "Can you imagine having to do everything with the wrong hand?"

"Grandma refused. The teacher told her unless she started using her right hand, she would never learn to write cursive. So she never did."

"Ever?"

"Have you ever seen her write in cursive?" Penina put her package next to Naomi's. Hers had a sticker shaped like a lamb. PENINA, it said across the flank. Naomi underlined the names with her finger. "That explains the no cursive," she said, "but why no small letters?"

Penina shrugged. "Don't know. Maybe for emphasis?"

Naomi peeled up the edge of her sticker-chick. "Let's see what we got," she said. She pulled off the whole chick without tearing it, and laid it next to her plate.

Penina picked at the lamb's ears. When she could slip her finger beneath the sticker, she pulled up gently. The lamb's head came up without tearing. Penina pulled a little more, and the lamb ripped in half, right across the first big N in PENINA.

88

Penina glanced at Naomi, but Naomi didn't look up. She peeled the tape off one end of her package and slid the gift out without tearing the paper.

It was a book.

The Secret Garden.

"Oh, Naomi, you're going to love it!" Penina said. "I read that last year with my neighbor." Once they started, all Penina and Zozo wanted to do was read it, or when they weren't reading it, talk about it. What was behind the locked door in the garden? Who was making the mysterious crying sound in the corridor? Barb and Barbara had been abandoned for weeks while Penina and Zozo read, discussed, and acted out *The Secret Garden*.

"Yeah," said Naomi, "I saw the movie when I was little, but I haven't read it yet. It looks good. What did you get?"

Penina turned the package over so Naomi wouldn't see what she'd done to the lamb. Hers was a book, too; that much was obvious. Maybe it would be another classic like the one Naomi had. Penina liked the heavy cover and the gold leaf on the edge of the pages. She tore off the paper and held up . . .

The Secret Garden.

"Hey, we match," Naomi said. She held up her hand for a high-five.

Penina tapped it flabbily. She already had *The Secret Garden.*

"Thank you, Grandma," Naomi called up the long table. "Thank you, Grandpa."

"Yeah, thanks. I really like it," Penina said. She'd been liking it for almost two years.

Grandma leaned toward them. "You're welcome, girls. I hope you enjoy it. That was my favorite book when I was your age."

Whose age? Naomi was a year younger than Penina. Sixteen months younger, actually. She was in fifth grade. Penina was almost in seventh. Grandma was about two years behind.

"What's wrong, Penina?" asked someone from way down at the end of the other table. "Why are you crying?"

"I'm not crying!" said Penina, even though she could feel her eyes and nose dripping. "I have to go to the bathroom."

"I think somebody is T-I-R-E-D," said a grown-up—a stupid grown-up if she thought Penina didn't know what T-I-R-E-D spelled.

Penina turned and ran.

"You know the drill," she said to herself in the bathroom mirror. "You cry, you go to the bathroom and wash your face. Then you hide there till Zozo comes to get you."

But Zozo was three hundred miles away. Maybe Naomi would come get her. Penina hoped not. That would be embarrassing. Naomi was only ten, and was she crying because she didn't like her *Afikoman* prize? Not at all.

Penina blew her nose and wiped her eyes. Crying

at the Seder, how babyish could you get? She washed her face, dried it on one of the fancy guest towels, and went back to the Seder.

"Penina-leh," said Daddy, "how are you feeling?"

"Fine."

"Do you want any more dessert?" asked Mom, pushing the macaroons toward Penina. "Once you eat the *Afikoman*, you can't eat anything else."

Penina shook her head. "No, thanks."

"Here," said Naomi, "I saved you some." She passed Penina a piece of matzah about as big as the ruined lamb sticker. Penina chewed it up and swallowed. It made her stomach feel better.

"Behold the cup of Elijah!" said Grandpa. Penina looked at the large silver goblet on the dining room table. It was filled to the top with dark red wine.

"According to legend, the Prophet Elijah travels from house to house on Passover and tastes a little of the wine in his cup."

Naomi yawned. That made Penina yawn, too. That made Naomi yawn again, and that made them both giggle.

"Children, will you please open the door for Elijah?" said Grandpa.

Penina and Naomi and the cousins and the neighbors walked to the front door. They opened the heavy wooden one, but left the screen door closed.

"Hey, Penina," said Daddy, when the kids came back to the table, "can Elijah come through a screen door?"

"I don't know, can he?" Penina said, but she did know. Daddy told this joke every year. It was her job to help.

"He can," Daddy said, "but it's a strain."

Everyone groaned, and Daddy gave Penina a friendly shoulder punch.

They sang *"Eliyahu Ha-navi,"* and it sounded even better than it had in the car. Then all the kids got up, shut the door, and sat back down.

"Look at Elijah's cup," said Grandma.

Some of the wine was gone.

"By the end of the night, Elijah is going to be blotto," said Grandma.

Penina put her chin on her hand and rested her elbow on the table.

Grandpa said a prayer in Hebrew. The grown-ups murmured, *"Aw-main."*

"Next year in Jerusalem," Grandpa said, and the grown-ups all said it back to him.

Penina folded her arms on the table. She wanted to put her head down, just for a minute. This Seder had gone on forever.

16. She Did What?

Something sure smelled good. Penina took a deep breath, but she didn't open her eyes. Not yet. She was snuggled too deep in a soft, floppy pillow for opening her eyes to seem like a good idea. She smelled cinnamon. And maple syrup. And something frying in butter. French toast? Penina opened her eyes.

Mimsy's face was all that she could see.

"Are you awake?" said Mimsy. "I've been up since seven, but Mommy said I couldn't wake you since you were up till almost midnight and you'd be cranky if you didn't get your rest, but I told her you'd be cranky anyway, even if I let you sleep all day, and Grandma's making *matzah brie*, which is like French toast but with matzah, and she said I could see if you were awake and wanted to come down and have brunch, which is like a cross between breakfast and lunch."

Penina pushed Mimsy out of the way and sat up.

94

She was in Grandma and Grandpa's house, in the room with the tan-and-beige striped wallpaper, in the bed by the dresser. Mimsy always got the bed by the wall.

"Okay, I'm coming," Penina said. "Let me get dressed first."

"You already are," said Mimsy.

Penina looked down at her nightgown. She wasn't wearing a nightgown. She was wearing her fancy green dress.

After breakfast, Penina opened her backpack, took out her homework folder, and got to work. She had about a thousand hours of homework ahead of her.

"She *what*?" Mom shouted.

Mom was downstairs, but Penina heard the question all the way up in the room with the tan-and-beige striped wallpaper. It was the kind of thing Mom said when someone was in trouble, and because Penina had been quietly studying—bothering no one—since she left the dining room, she thought there was a good chance the person in trouble might not be her.

"That can't be true. She would have told me." Mom's voice easily made it to the second floor.

Penina heard Grandma's voice, but she couldn't tell what she was saying. She wasn't shouting like Mom was.

"Penina! Come down here," Mom called.

Penina got up slowly. She put her worksheets in her folder and put the folder in her backpack. She put her pencil in the backpack's little front pocket. This couldn't be about anything she'd done, could it? Maybe Mimsy was in trouble, and Penina was being summoned to testify against her.

Downstairs, Mom, Dad, Grandma, and Grandpa stood side by side, like a row of teeth, like a panel of judges, like the Pittsburgh Steelers' defensive line. Mom asked, "Did Ms. Anderson make you write a letter as the Easter Bunny?"

"No," Penina said. Ms. Anderson had *tried* to make her write a letter as the Easter Bunny, but Penina never did.

"Penina, darling, tell your parents what you told me in the kitchen yesterday," Grandma said. She sat down on the couch and patted the cushion beside her. Everyone took seats around the living room and waited for Penina to speak.

"My teacher taught us a song about a bunny!" Mimsy shouted. She stood up in the middle of the room and belted out, "Little Bunny Foo Foo, hopping through the forest—"

"Sit down, Mimsy," Mom said. Penina thought she should circle this date on the calendar: the first time in the history of the world that her mother had told Mimsy to be quiet so Mom could listen to Penina.

She told them all about the Easter Bunny letter—how Zozo had tried to help her, how Ryan had blushed bright red under pressure, how she had flushed the yellow stationery in the girls' room before she went to lunch.

"When was this?" asked Dad.

"Um, last week, the day I was grounded," said Penina, "the first day."

"Why didn't you tell us?" Mom asked.

"I don't know," Penina said. Because I thought you'd be angry, Penina thought. And she'd been right. Mom's face looked the same way it had when Daisy left them a headless brown rat on their back porch a few weeks ago.

"Sonia," Grandma said, "I told Penina how proud I was of her, refusing to do something against her conscience."

"Of course," said Daddy, "we're proud of Penina."

"Very proud," said Mom, but she still looked like she was viewing a dead rat. "Ms. Anderson had no right to base her class work on the Easter Bunny," she told Penina.

"Or to single you out the way she did," said Dad.

Mom stood up. "I'm going to call her. I'm going

to tell her to stick to teaching my child reading, writing, and arithmetic. I send my daughter to school to get an education. I do not send her to receive religious indoctrination."

Two big steps brought Mom to the phone in the corner. "You know," she said, "in some school districts, a teacher could be fired for that kind of cultural insensitivity."

Mom picked up the phone and punched in three numbers. "Yes. Marionville School, please, in Marionville, Pennsylvania."

Penina jumped up after her. She tried to push the hang-up button, but this was a different kind of phone. The button was on the receiver in Mom's hand.

"No, Mom, please don't," Penina begged.

Mom bent her head to face Penina. The dead-rat look was gone. Mom looked surprised and—maybe, Penina wasn't sure—a little frightened. "Why not?"

"Ms. Anderson will think I'm a tattletale."

Mom looked away. She said to the phone, "No, thank you." It beeped when she hung it up.

"Discussing your schoolwork with your parents is not tattling, Penina," Grandpa said. He sat in his big recliner, hands laced across his middle.

Dad leaned toward Penina. "Ms. Anderson is a new

98

teacher. She's still learning how to run her classroom. Let us talk to her. We'll explain she can't make her classroom an unwelcoming place for her students."

"Educator to educator," said Mom. "Just teachers talking shop."

"Mom, Dad, please don't call her. She already hates me. If you yell at her for something she did to me, that's just going to make it worse." Penina glanced at Mimsy, sitting on the floor near Grandpa's chair, curls boinging all over the place.

Mom put the phone back in its holder. "All right. We won't call Ms. Anderson. We'll talk about this some more later on. Right now, it's time for you to get a little fresh air. Go play outside with Mimsy, but stay in the yard. The guests for the second Seder will be here soon."

The guests were just some grown-up friends of Grandma and Grandpa's. Naomi was at her other grandparents' house tonight. The second Seder wasn't as fancy or as long as the first one, but it still went pretty late. Penina didn't get to bed till nearly eleven, and she slept in the car almost all the way back the next day.

17. Snails and Frogs' Legs

"You were gone forever! You missed so much!" said Zozo. The Window Phone was best at night. Everything was dark, except for the bright square of Window Phone, where Zozo was holding her arms out wide to show Penina how much she had missed. "Barbara ventured into the lair of the giant prowler and was almost eaten alive."

"Thanks for taking care of Daisy," Penina said.

"That's okay, but listen. You missed a ton of stuff. First of all, Dr. Tobin came in to talk to us."

"Why?" The last time Dr. Tobin had come to their classroom, it was to announce that Mrs. Brown was leaving. Maybe Ms. Anderson was leaving, too. Maybe she was getting married, and her honeymoon was a trip around the world, so she wouldn't be back before the end of the school year. Maybe she had quit her job at Marionville School and signed up to tutor circus children in Beijing. Maybe she had some kind of illness, nothing life-threatening, but maybe a sty or a spreading rash that would keep her out of school for a couple of months.

"He gave us this big talk about how we were all special, and how every one of us should be proud of our heritage."

"He did?" How was that worth a special visit from the principal? Penina remembered her conversation with her parents. Mom had promised not to call Ms. Anderson, but she hadn't said anything about calling Dr. Tobin. "Was he mad?"

"No, just real serious. Then Ms. Anderson said we were starting a new unit on diversity—you know, our different backgrounds, where our grandparents came from, and stuff like that."

But they weren't supposed to start a new unit on diversity—or anything else—this week. Penina had gotten her assignments in advance so she could do them while she was away. She had a chapter in her Language Arts book and a worksheet about the metric system, but there hadn't been anything about diversity.

"Did Ms. Anderson seem upset, like, maybe Dr. Tobin was *making* her do a unit on diversity?" said Penina.

Zozo leaned on the glass on her side of the

Window Phone, as if she were trying to get a better look at Penina. "I don't know. Maybe. She kept telling us to 'Focus, people!' but she always does that."

"Zozo, this is important. When did Dr. Tobin talk to you?"

"Um, yesterday?" said Zozo, but she didn't sound sure. "Yeah, Wednesday," she added, and this time Penina could tell she meant it. "I remember, because I was wearing a ponytail."

Yeah, Wednesday was ponytail-in-the-back day. Two side ponies today: it must be Thursday.

Monday   Tuesday   Wednesday   Thursday   Friday

"He came in at the end of Language Arts and didn't leave till the early-bus bell. We missed all of Social Studies," Zozo said.

Penina concentrated. Language Arts was over around 1:30. At 1:30 on Wednesday, Penina had been climbing the willow tree in Grandma and Grandpa's yard. Had Mom called Dr. Tobin after the Big Talk?

"Penina, why do you care?" Zozo rapped her knuckles on the window, and Penina thought she heard a very faint knocking sound.

"Well, you said I missed a ton of stuff. What else was there?"

"Ms. Anderson told us to bring in something from our heritage. I'm going to bring in the little Persian rug from the guest room and a letter my grandfather wrote in Farsi."

"*Salaam,*" said Penina. It was the first Farsi word Zozo had taught her. It meant hello.

"*Salaam,*" Zozo said back. "So, anyway, today we spent the whole day planning what we are going to bring in and making diversity posters."

Penina wondered what she should bring in. A Seder plate? A box of matzah? Maybe she could bring in a whole sponge cake with strawberry topping. She would give it all to Ms. Anderson and explain that Mom had called Dr. Tobin on her own; Penina had nothing to do with it.

"So Anne is bringing a Claddaugh ring, which she says is a symbol of Ireland," said Zozo, "and Jackie says her mom has this fancy cloth from Ghana, where her ancestors were from. And, like, half the class is German, so they had to make sure they

104

weren't all bringing the same thing. Suzie said she could bring in a German cuckoo clock, which no one else was bringing, but guess what Ryan is going to bring?"

Penina had no idea.

"Guess," said Zozo. "Here's a hint. It's not a *what*. It's a *who*."

The Easter Bunny?

"His grandmother!"

"That's nice," said Penina.

"She's from France. She probably eats snails and frogs' legs. Maybe she'll bring some. Maybe she'll make us eat them!"

"Uh-huh," Penina said. She'd rather eat snails and frogs' legs than face Ms. Anderson. Because if Mom had yelled at Dr. Tobin, and if Dr. Tobin had yelled at Ms. Anderson, Ms. Anderson was going to be mad. At Penina.

18. Crazy

Mom and Dad were still up. Penina could hear their TV. She walked down the hall to their bedroom and pushed open their door.

"Did you call Dr. Tobin?" she asked.

Mom and Dad looked at her, at each other, and back at her again.

"Penina, it's almost midnight. You need your sleep," said Dad.

Mom clicked off the TV.

"Did you call Dr. Tobin from Grandma and Grandpa's house? After you promised not to call Ms. Anderson? Did you, Mom?"

"Well, no," Mom said. She took a deep breath. "But—"

"I did," said Dad. "Your mother and I talked about it, and we decided we didn't want you returning to a hostile classroom environment."

"So you called the principal?" Penina couldn't

believe it. She didn't think getting in trouble with Dr. Tobin was going to make Ms. Anderson any less hostile.

"Shh. Don't wake Mimsy," Mom whispered.

Dad said, "I know Dr. Tobin. We taught together when I was at Ellsworth Elementary, before he became a principal."

About a million years ago. Penina had been a baby. Mimsy hadn't even been born yet.

"We trust Dr. Tobin to handle this with sensitivity," said Mom.

"He's a *mensch*," said Dad. "A decent human being."

"I know what *mensch* means," Penina reminded him.

"How'd you know we'd talked to him?" said Dad.

"Well, gee"—Penina paced and recounted the evidence—"Dr. Tobin gives a talk on respecting differences on the very same day my mother and father threaten to call. Everyone drops what they're doing to make diversity posters. Did my parents have anything to do with all this? Let me just take a wild guess here: Yes!"

"Penina, keep your voice down," said Dad.

Penina stomped her foot. That wasn't loud enough, so she jumped up and came down hard, twice. "I *am* keeping my voice down!" she shouted. They were missing the point. This was not about being quiet. They had called the school. They had ruined her life.

"That's enough. You'll wake your sister." Mom's eyes were gray, and they were riveted on Penina. Steel gray, thought Penina. This must be what they meant when they said someone had a *steely gaze*. Would it work with brown eyes, too? Penina's eyes were brown. She tried to return Mom's steely gaze.

"So, yeah," said Penina, "when Zozo told me what was going on at school, I kind of figured you had called, even though you said you wouldn't." Penina was steely. Penina was sneery. Let them explain why they had lied to her. She wasn't going to back down.

"Did you hear that?" said Mom. She wasn't even looking at Penina. She was looking at Dad. Smiling at him.

He was smiling back. "Yes, I did. Our little girl is growing up."

"She's practically a teenager," said Mom.

She was practically twelve. What was *wrong* with these people?

"I remember when I first started getting sarcastic with my parents," said Mom. "I was just about Penina's age."

They pushed down their covers and got out of bed. Zozo's mother slept in short, silky nighties.

Penina was glad her mother didn't do that. Tonight, Mom and Dad had on matching gray sweats and tees. They were coming at her, one on each side.

"What are you doing?" Penina yelled, tried to yell, but she couldn't. She couldn't say a thing. She couldn't see a thing. The whole world had turned into nothing but gray T-shirt material, the smell of fabric softener, and the voices of these big, crazy maniacs who wouldn't stop hugging her.

19. Pizza Day

Cheese cubes. Grapes. A jelly sandwich on matzah. Penina imagined the food packed snugly in her purple lunch bag in her locker in the hallway. Ms. Anderson was pointing to a world map and saying the names of countries across the ocean, but Penina barely noticed. She planned to eat the cheese cubes first, then the jelly sandwich, and save the grapes for last. No, she would eat one grape, one cheese cube, one grape, one cheese cube until they were all gone, then she would eat the jelly sandwich.

Her stomach growled. It was just a little grumble; Penina didn't think anyone else could hear it. She pictured the sides of her empty stomach rubbing together, growling and grumbling.

Ms. Anderson wrote vocabulary words on the board in blue marker: *Ancestors. Genealogy.* She didn't seem upset about Dad's phone call to Dr. Tobin. She hadn't yelled or snarled or anything. When Penina turned in her thick homework folder, Ms. Anderson just thanked her and smiled. Maybe Dr. Tobin hadn't told Ms. Anderson the whole story. Maybe he had, and Ms. Anderson was waiting for the right moment to get back at Penina. The marker squeaked on the whiteboard. *Heritage. Immigration.*

There was a sound like the one Daisy made when she didn't want to be held, *grrrrrr*. It was Penina's stomach, impatient for lunch. The kids sitting near her looked at her and giggled.

"Okay, people, let's see a little maturity around here. Everyone has a stomach. Get over it."

Penina crunched into her pencil and mentally thanked Ms. Anderson for sticking up for her. Everyone did have a stomach, even Ms. Anderson. Hers was probably full of oats, apples, sugar cubes: pony food.

Doors slammed, and the hallway filled with footsteps and voices. It was the seventh graders, going to the cafeteria.

Penina's stomach lost its mind. *Grr! Gurgle! Blub!* Yes! Time for lunch! Finally!

Friday was Pizza Day, so Penina and Zozo were practically the only ones in the whole entire school who didn't line up to buy lunch. They grabbed the big round table by the window and saved seats for Anne and Jackie.

Penina ripped open the Velcro top of her lunch bag. She pulled out a clear plastic container of grapes, green ones. She'd eaten half of them before Zozo had even finished unwrapping her food. Penina was starving.

"Wow. Chicken. I'm stunned," said Zozo, obviously not stunned at all. She had chicken roll-ups every day. It was practically the only food in the world she wasn't allergic to. She dropped the roll-up on the table and leaned back in her chair with her arms crossed.

"No muffin?" asked Penina, once she'd swallowed another grape.

"No. Mom didn't bake yet this week. I've got gluten-free pretzels instead." She scooted a bag over to Penina.

"No, thanks. They're not KP. Want some grapes?"

Zozo took a grape and stashed it in her cheek. "What's *KP*?"

"Kosher for Passover. Nothing leavened." Penina unwrapped her cheese cubes and offered one to Zozo.

Zozo shook her head. Penina remembered that Zozo couldn't have cheese. Or milk. Or anything made with milk.

"How come you guys aren't having the pizza?" Ms. Anderson asked.

Zozo didn't answer. Neither did Penina. It seemed

112

like a lot to explain. And besides, what was Ms. Anderson doing here? Shouldn't she be eating on the teachers' side? With the teachers?

"You are so missing out!" Ms. Anderson said. "Okay if I sit here?" She sat down and took a bite of pizza and a swig of milk, no straw. "How was your Seder, Penina?"

"Fine."

Did Ms. Anderson want a report? An essay— "Penina's Peekskill Passover"?

"Anne! Jackie!" yelled Zozo. She jumped up and waved big arcs with both arms. Penina looked where Zozo was looking. Anne and Jackie had just gotten through the cafeteria line. "Come here! We saved seats for you!" Zozo called.

Jackie and Anne and their trays of pizza crossed the cafeteria to the big round table. They gave Zozo and Penina looks of, *What's going on?*

"Sit with us," said Penina. Zozo had the right idea. The more the merrier. Let Ms. Anderson quiz *them*.

"Well, we kind of promised Suzie," Anne mumbled.

"We saved you seats," Zozo said. She smacked the seat next to her. "Sit here."

Anne and Jackie looked at each other, shrugged, and sat.

Penina popped a cheese cube into her mouth and

113

chewed slowly so she wouldn't have to talk for a while. She took out her jelly-on-matzah and put every ounce of attention she had into unwrapping it. She was absorbed, concentrating, much too busy to have a conversation with Ms. Anderson.

"So, did you eat the bitter herbs?" Ms. Anderson asked. Penina tore her attention away from the plastic wrap. Ms. Anderson was smiling right at her. "That's my favorite part. My brother and I used to see who could eat the biggest spoonful without crying."

Was Ms. Anderson Jewish? Penina didn't think she was. Kristine Anderson wasn't exactly a Jewish name, but then, neither was Ryan O'Connor, and he was in Penina's own religious school class at Temple Beth Shalom.

"Are you Jewish?" asked Zozo.

"Nope, Presbyterian. But my church puts on a Seder every Passover," Ms. Anderson said. She had a tiny dot of pizza sauce on her cheek, like an extra-red freckle.

"She's probably been to more Seders than you have, Penina," said Zozo.

So, what? Now Ms. Anderson was some kind of Seder expert?

"Well, I don't know about that," Ms. Anderson said. She was smiling at Penina like they were suddenly best friends, Seder buddies. "But I've been to a few, enough to know they're really special. That's why I was so surprised when this whole Easter Bunny letter turned out to be such a big deal. I wasn't trying to make you celebrate Easter, Penina. I just wanted to include you in something special, something fun."

Was Ms. Anderson apologizing? Not exactly, but she was trying to be nice. It was like the teacher version of Zozo's eyelash flutters.

"I know," Penina said. *Now* she knew, since Ms. Anderson explained it to her, but it hadn't felt like something special at the time, and that zero in the grade book, that wasn't exactly tons of fun.

"I'm sorry if I came across as not respecting your religion," Ms. Anderson said. "Believe me, that's the last thing I wanted to do."

Now she *was* apologizing. Sort of. She'd said the words "I'm sorry," but she'd also said "if." Ms. Anderson still didn't get it. Penina wanted to paint it on the wall in red capital letters, to announce it over the school's public address system, to scream it into Ms. Anderson's ear until she finally understood: *You told me to do an impossible assignment. You embarrassed me in front of the class. You gave me a zero. That was wrong! That was unfair! That was mean!*

"Okay," she said instead. After all, the teacher had apologized.

"Great!" Ms. Anderson yelled. She looked so happy that for a minute Penina thought she was going to lead them in a sing-along or something, but she just took a big bite of pizza and chewed enthusiastically.

"How do you like the pizza?" asked Jackie. She'd probably been hoping for a normal lunch. Maybe she thought she could still have one.

"Delicious!" said Ms. Anderson. She'd eaten three slices, except the crusts. The crusts were lined up along the side of her tray. "I shouldn't have it, though. Now I'm definitely going to break out. I'm twenty-four years old, but my skin thinks I'm fourteen."

Anne giggled. "My skin thinks I'm fourteen, and I'm only eleven." What a teacher's pet.

Penina didn't want her cheese cubes. She was done with her grapes. She poked at her jelly sandwich, but she couldn't eat it. It was crushed and too crumbly to hold together.

"We've got a guest speaker today, guys. I better go back and get set up," said Ms. Anderson, finally.

"Here, let me take your tray," said Anne.

"Take mine, too?" said Jackie. Maybe she wasn't

116

thrilled with Anne's new suck-up-to-Ms. Anderson attitude.

"It was great having lunch together!" said Ms. Anderson. She slid her tray to Anne. She leaned over close to Penina and smiled. Penina caught a whiff of pizza sauce and wintergreen gum. "We're good on that Easter Bunny thing now, right?" Ms. Anderson asked, quietly.

Penina knew there were some words you didn't say at school, and later, looking back, she would wonder why she didn't just use an acceptable word, like *nonsense* or *baloney*. But when Ms. Anderson smiled at her, as if the Easter Bunny letter had never really meant anything, as if it had all been a silly misunderstanding, as if she and Penina were the greatest pals in the world, Penina couldn't stop to think of another way to say "I disagree." Instead, she shouted the first word that came into her head.

It was an eight-letter word beginning with *B*. It meant the waste product of a large, horned farm animal, and it turned out to be a much worse thing to say than *shut up*.

20. Deep Trouble

Penina was back in the green chair outside Dr. Tobin's office. This time she didn't have to *pretend* to be a bad kid. She was in trouble, deep trouble. Deep, dark, thick, smelly trouble.

"Penina, come in," said Dr. Tobin.

He sat down at his desk, and Penina sat across from him. He had the messiest desk Penina had ever seen. It was covered in papers and folders and coffee mugs and a zillion multicolored sticky notes.

"You know," said Dr. Tobin in his bass-drum voice, "the First Amendment grants us freedom of expression, but that right does not extend to every type of speech."

Penina nodded. Maybe Dr. Tobin would get so caught up in his lecture he'd forget why Penina was in trouble. It happened that way with Dad sometimes.

"Slander is not protected. Neither is sedition— advocating the overthrow of the government. And

119

I'm afraid the obscenity you pronounced for Ms. Anderson is not protected, either. I'm sure you understand why that sort of language is not permitted in school."

Penina nodded again. She leaned back a little in her seat. Dr. Tobin didn't seem angry, more like he wanted to have a reasonable discussion of school rules. Dad was right about Dr. Tobin. He was a *mensch*.

"So, I'm going to call and explain the situation to your parents." He lifted the receiver and pushed a button on the phone. Penina could hear the dial tone all the way across the desk.

"You don't have to do that!" Penina yelled. She realized she was yelling and made herself speak in a regular voice. "I mean, wouldn't it be easier for you just to send a note? I promise I'll give it to them. And, besides, if you call my dad, the school's just going to put you on hold forever. A note won't waste your time." Her voice sounded tinny and timid, like she didn't have enough air to push out the words. Her sides hurt. She'd been trying to hold her breath and talk at the same time.

"Sit down, Penina."

Penina sat. She hadn't realized she'd been standing. Dr. Tobin pulled a pink sticky note off his computer monitor. It had Penina's home phone number on it.

He punched the numbers on his phone. Penina felt her heartbeat in her throat, in her chest, in her stomach.

"Hello, this is Dr. Tobin calling from Marionville School. May I please speak with your mother?"

Mimsy! She should have known Mimsy would answer the phone. Maybe this was good. The way Mimsy talked, she'd keep the line tied up until dismissal. Penina would be home before Dr. Tobin ever got through to her mother.

"That's right. I'm your sister's principal. Will you ask your mother to come to the phone?"

Penina could barely hear Mimsy's side of the conversation, but it was clear she was chattering on about something. Dr. Tobin looked amused, then bored, then impatient. Penina remembered to breathe.

"I need to speak with your mother. Please give her the telephone," Dr. Tobin said, then, after a moment, "Hello, Sonia, it's Tom. Yes, she's fine. As a matter of fact, she is right here in my office."

It was weird that he was using their first names.

"Well, I'm afraid she lost her temper and used language inappropriate for the school setting."

It was weird that he was talking about her as if she weren't even there.

"I trust you to do so. In addition, the school disciplinary code calls for detention in cases such as this."

121

Detention. In the LAC, the Learning Adjustment Center. With the bad kids, kids who took your notebook and drew gross things on the cover, kids who whispered nasty remarks about you and snickered. Zozo and Ryan and Jackie and Anne and everyone would be out in the fresh springtime air, laughing, playing H-O-R-S-E, but Penina would be imprisoned in the hot, stinky LAC. She couldn't believe it.

"Of course you can," said Dr. Tobin. He held the phone out to Penina. "Your mother would like to speak to you."

Penina took the phone. It was warm where Dr. Tobin had held it. Or maybe Mom's anger was pulsing through the fiber-optic cable, heating up the receiver. Penina took a deep breath. "Hello?" she said.

"Hello, Penina." Mom's voice was solemn, like a meteorologist's announcing a massive blizzard. "I'm sorry to hear about this. We'll talk about it when you get home. Are you all right?"

"Yes," Penina answered, and it wasn't until then that she started to cry.

21. Twelve Little Girls in Two Straight Lines

Penina held the hand with the phone straight out at Dr. Tobin, and clamped the other one over her eyes. If she couldn't push the tears back in, at least she could hide them.

Dr. Tobin took back the phone. "I think she will be fine. Yes, I know you do. Of course, please call any time. Thank you. Good-bye."

Penina heard the quiet click of the phone hanging up. She dropped her hand, sniffled, and looked up at Dr. Tobin. He shifted things around on his desk and uncovered a squashed square box of tissues. He offered it to Penina. She took two. He dug around on his desk some more and offered her a bowl of wrapped butterscotch candies. Penina shook her head. More digging, more offers: a Handi Wipe, a cough drop, a pencil with a neon green pom-pom where the eraser should have been.

That one made Penina giggle, and she blew a bubble out her nose. "Oh!" she yelped, and grabbed a couple more tissues.

"I know it's hard to keep your temper, Penina," Dr. Tobin said. "It's something I struggle with on a daily basis."

Penina checked Dr. Tobin's face. Was he struggling with his temper right now? No, he was back to lecturing. "Learning self-control is an ongoing process, but it does get easier with practice."

Penina snuck a glance at the clock above the doorway. More than two hours till dismissal. That wasn't fair. It felt like she'd been in Dr. Tobin's office forever. School should have been over by now. She should leave the principal's office, go outside, and look up to see the moon and stars in a black sky. It should be at least midnight. It should already be tomorrow.

"Mrs. Mulrane will give you a pass to take back to your classroom. You have a remarkable guest speaker this afternoon. You'll want to give her your full attention, so let's put this episode behind us." Dr. Tobin stood up and opened the door for Penina.

Penina's classroom was about five hundred miles away at the other end of the hallway. She took her time getting there. She made sure all the tears and sniffles and hiccups had stopped. She took a drink at

124

the water fountain and thought about stopping in the girls' room for a minute. She was still making up her mind when she heard quick footsteps clicking down the hallway. She turned and watched a petite lady in a fur jacket and high-heeled boots coming toward her.

The lady gave Penina a smile and a little wave as she walked by. She was followed by a scent of something nice, roses or lilac. Penina watched her walk away, down to the end of the hallway, where she turned left, into Penina's classroom.

The guest speaker? "Oh, yeah," Penina exclaimed to the empty hallway. Ryan's grandmother was coming to visit their class. That must be her.

Penina slipped into her seat without giving Ms. Anderson the hall pass. The teacher was busy hanging up the lady's fur jacket.

"You're back!" Zozo squeezed Penina's arm with both hands. "I thought you'd been expelled! What happened?"

Before Penina could answer, Ms. Anderson announced, "Class, I'd like you to welcome Mrs. Friedberg, Ryan's grandmother."

Everybody clapped, and Penina hoped the noise would cover her whisper to Zozo. "I'll tell you after school." She'd been in enough trouble for one day. Best to lay low for a while.

"Good afternoon," said Mrs. Friedberg. Penina stared. Her grandmothers just looked like regular grandmothers. Ryan's grandmother looked like a countess. From her black hair styled in a knot at the back of her neck, to her matching pearl necklace and earrings, to her neat round fingernails, painted pale pink, everything about her looked like royalty.

She sounded like a countess, too. For instance, she said "zat" for "that" when she told them, "I am Mrs. Friedberg, but I wish zat you would call me Evaline."

Ms. Anderson offered Evaline a chair, but she sat down on top of the teacher's desk. Penina had never

seen a grown-up do that before. Evaline uncapped a green bottle of fizzy water and took a sip. She placed it next to her on the desk and said, "I am a Holocaust survivor. My family lived near Nice, in the south of France. When I was nine years old, our town was occupied by the Nazis."

Penina felt a chill. She knew about the Nazis: How they started in Germany and took over lots of other countries. How they caused World War Two. How they killed millions and millions of people. How they hated Jews. They killed six million Jews. It was called the Holocaust.

Evaline continued, "They sent my father and brothers to the death camps, but my mother found a way to protect me. She enrolled me in a boarding school run by nuns. If anyone there found out I was a Jew, the nuns could have gone to prison. I could have been sent to the death camps. So, I had to pretend to be Catholic."

Evaline crossed her ankles, smoothed her skirt. "It was very difficult because I did not know anything about Catholicism, and I was very young."

Penina imagined living in a French boarding school, having to do everything with eleven other girls in two straight lines, like in *Madeline*.

"My first morning at the new school, I ate a big

breakfast," Evaline said. "Maybe I should have been too lonesome and worried to eat, but I was a growing girl, and I was hungry." She clapped her hands over her tummy. Penina laughed a little at that, then bit down hard on her lip to stop. She didn't want Evaline to think she was laughing at her.

"After breakfast, we went to chapel—church. I had never been to church before, but I just did the same things as the other girls, and I thought I fit right in."

Penina pictured twelve little girls going to church in two straight lines.

"Soon, some of the girls got up and stood in line in front of the priest. I didn't want to go, but I thought if I didn't do it, I would call attention to myself. So, I stood up and got in line. All of a sudden, my classmates, my teacher, the other nuns, everyone in the chapel, it seemed to me, was tapping on my shoulders, tugging on my dress, saying, 'No, no! What are you doing? You can't take communion. You just had breakfast!'"

Evaline pressed her hands to her cheeks and turned pink. That must be where Ryan got his blushfulness.

"I didn't know you couldn't take communion on a full stomach. I didn't even know what communion was. I just knew I had ruined my hiding place. Now everyone would know I wasn't Catholic. I'd be kicked out, and my mother would be so disappointed."

Evaline stopped and sipped her bubbly water. Penina shivered. She snuck a glance at Ryan. He was proof. The Nazis hadn't gotten Evaline. She'd grown up. She had a grandson.

"What happened, Mrs. Friedberg?" Penina whispered. She felt that ache in her forehead again, that tickle in her nose. She knew what that meant, but she didn't run away. She listened.

Evaline slid off the desk and paced the front of the room. "Nothing," she said. "I went back to my pew and sat down. Nobody ever mentioned it again. I think they must have known, but they never betrayed me. They risked their freedom, they risked their *lives*, to protect me."

Evaline walked to Ryan's desk and put her hand on his shoulder. He smiled at her (and blushed, of course). "After the war, my mother and I came to America. I grew up, got married, and had two girls. And now, I have a handsome grandson I can embarrass in front of his friends."

Evaline put one hand on each side of her grandson's face. She leaned down and put about ten thousand kisses on top of Ryan's red head. He didn't look embarrassed, though. He looked proud.

22. Immature and Rude

"Penina! Pen! Ni! Na!" yelled Zozo. If she was shouting to get Penina's attention, it worked. She didn't have to pinch her, too.

"Hey," said Penina, "cut it out." She hugged her arm and rubbed the sore spot, but she didn't stop walking. She and Zozo had already gone all but one block. They'd be home in a minute.

"Well, quit ignoring me, and I'll quit pinching you," said Zozo. "Why won't you answer me?"

Penina didn't remember the question. She'd been thinking about Ryan's grandmother. "Sorry, Zozo. What did you say?"

Zozo sighed and rolled her eyes. "I said, 'Barbara and Barb should explore the desert region today, and you can tell me what happened with Dr. Tobin.' I said it fifty times, but you wouldn't even look at me. What's wrong with you?"

The desert region was Zozo's old sandbox. Penina

didn't want to take Barb and Barbara out today.

"Nothing," said Penina, "I was just thinking. Do you think Mrs. Friedberg already knew when she went to that school that her father and brothers were dead, or do you think she found out later, after the war?"

They took a few steps before Zozo answered. "I don't know. Later, I guess. She probably hoped she'd see them again."

Zozo and Penina walked slowly, even though they were almost home.

"It was really nice of those nuns to protect her," Penina said.

"They had to," Zozo said. "It was part of their religion."

Zozo's house was twenty-three steps closer to school than Penina's, so Zozo got home first, but she didn't go in right away. "Is your mom going to be mad?" she said. "Do you want me to come in with you?"

That was the thing about Zozo. One minute she was pinching you on the arm, the next she was offering to get between you and your angry mother. "Thanks, Zozo. You don't have to do that. She seemed all right on the phone."

"Okay. Good luck. I'll call you later."

Penina watched her get the mail from the mailbox and take it in with her. Penina's mailbox was already empty; so was the front hall and the kitchen.

"Penina's home!" yelled Mimsy. She came running in from the den in a yellow tutu and a brown-and-green straw hat. "Penina, I'm the Tansy Fairy from your flower fairy book! Your principal called, and I talked to him, and I told him I'm the Tansy Fairy, and he said he wanted to talk to Mommy."

Penina patted Mimsy on the crown of her hat and went upstairs.

"Penina! You're home!" Mom met her in the hallway and gave her a squeeze around the shoulders. "Now, I know you're upset. You're going through a hard time right now, but I want you to know, Daddy and I love you, and we'll do whatever we can to help you. Do you understand?"

No, thought Penina, I don't understand. I don't understand at all. How can you help? Can you bring back Evaline's father and brothers? Can you protect me from the bad kids in the LAC? Can you give Ms. Anderson the *first clue* about why I am never, ever going to write that stupid Easter Bunny letter? No, you can't. You can't do anything, so why don't you just leave me alone?

"Yeah, I know," Penina said. She shrugged under

Mom's arm. If Mom would just let go of her, she could put down her backpack. It weighed about ten tons.

Thud. There was the sound of something falling in the kitchen, and Mimsy shouted, "Mom! Come here! Daisy knocked over the coffeemaker!"

Penina would have bet a Sacagawea dollar Mimsy had knocked over the coffeemaker herself. Daisy was probably outside or under Penina's bed. Poor cat, but at least Mimsy couldn't blame the coffeemaker's fall on Penina. Penina had an air-tight alibi.

"I'll be right back," said Mom. She went downstairs, and Penina went to her room.

Penina opened her backpack and pulled out her take-home folder. She opened her take-home folder and found Alan's Easter-wish letter at the back. She sat at her desk and got out a notebook and her best gel pen.

Dear Alan, She wrote. She didn't bother with her neatest handwriting, didn't bother with the date.

There's no such thing as the Easter Bunny. It's all a big lie. And by the way, jelly dino eggs rot your teeth.
Sincerely,
Penina Levine

Penina crumpled up the letter and threw it away. She didn't need to be mean to Alan. Besides, that wasn't even what she meant. She turned to a new piece of paper and started again.

Dear Alan,

She crossed it out.

Dear Ms. Anderson,

Penina sighed. Yeah, that was better. If Ms. Anderson wouldn't listen to Penina, maybe she would *read* what Penina had to say.

I'm sorry I said an impolite word to you. It was immature and rude, and I won't do it again.

Penina thought about writing "I promise," but she decided against it. She hadn't meant to say it the first time. How could she be sure not to do it again? She'd try, but she wouldn't promise.

I know you didn't mean to make me feel bad with the Easter Bunny assignment. You meant to include me in something fun, but it made me feel like you

Penina tried about thirty different ways to finish the letter, but she crossed them all out.

like you thought everyone should celebrate Easter.

like you were forcing me to be someone I'm not.

134

like you don't like Jews very much.

Penina capped the gel pen. She had a headache. Her throat hurt. She'd get some orange juice and finish this up later.

23. Tastes Like Snot

"Hey, Mimsy, come here," said Penina. Her voice sounded like a frog's, like a snake's, like the hinges on a heavy door to a dark, dusty room in an abandoned mansion.

"Yeah?" Mimsy ran in and barreled into the couch. Penina sat up so they wouldn't bump heads, and the whole room tilted and swayed. She closed her eyes to get it to stop.

"Are you still sick, Pina?" Mimsy yelled.

"Mmm-hmm," Penina answered. She had a headache and a stuffy nose and a ratchety catch in her chest. She was about 75 percent sure she wasn't going to make it. It wasn't the flu that was going to kill her, though. It was the boredom.

"You want to help me write my will?" Penina asked her sister. It wasn't like Penina was *playing* with Mimsy. She would never do that. This was something important that needed to be done before she passed from this world. Besides, Zozo was at school. Daisy was out hunting. Mom was in her office in the attic. Dad was at work, and she'd seen every DVD in the house at least ten thousand times.

"Who is Will?" Mimsy shouted. She was bouncing on the couch by Penina's feet. Penina pressed on her shoulders to make her sit still.

"It's not a who. It's a what. It's so Mom and Dad will know what to do with my stuff when I die."

"When are you going to die?" asked Mimsy. It was like she was asking, "When are you going to Peekskill?" She didn't look even a tiny bit worried, just curious. *Wide-eyed*, Penina guessed it was called, because Mimsy's eyes were big and round and so wide-open Penina wondered what was keeping them from popping right out of her face.

"I don't know," Penina answered. She stopped to cough for a little while, not for the drama of it, but because she really had to. "But it might be soon. I've been very sick." She blew her nose and threw away the tissue. It landed on top of a mound of tissues piled up around the wastebasket. Penina's aim wasn't perfect. "Go get me a pencil and some paper," she said.

Mimsy dashed out and dashed back with a purple marker and three pieces of orange construction paper. Fine. Penina would recopy it onto lined paper later.

"Now, write this down," she said. "The Last Will and Testament of Penina Levine."

"How do you spell 'the'?" asked Mimsy.

Penina spelled it. Mimsy made the letters all caps, like Grandma's.

"How do you spell 'last'?" asked Mimsy.

"Never mind," said Penina. This was going to take forever. She leaned back against her big, furry pillow. It wasn't really a pillow. It was Elgy, on loan from Mimsy. Mimsy had kept insisting he would make Penina feel better until Penina finally gave in and put the bear behind her to lean on. Barb was back there, too, tucked beneath Elgy's chin.

"Sing the 'Meow Song,'" said Mimsy.

What *meow* song? Oh, yeah, she meant "Bicycle Built for Two," Daisy's version. "I can't sing, Mimsy. I can barely talk."

"You're talking now," Mimsy corrected her.

Penina started to answer but coughed instead. She didn't even care if she coughed on Mimsy. Mimsy never got sick. Not even germs could stand being around her for very long.

Nothing bad ever happened to Mimsy. She never got sick. She never got bored. She never got grounded. That's how it had always been, that's how

138

it always would be. Penina tried to picture Mimsy as a sixth grader. What if Ms. Anderson was still teaching in seven years? What if she tried to make Mimsy do something Mimsy didn't want to do? It would be like King Kong versus Godzilla, like Dracula versus Frankenstein, like Snow White's evil stepmother versus the Wicked Witch of the West.

But Mimsy would win. Penina was certain. Mimsy would know exactly how to handle Ms. Anderson. She wouldn't even have to think about it.

"Hey, Mimsy," said Penina. She cleared her throat and continued, "Go get my backpack. It's up in my room, next to my desk. Bring it down here."

Mimsy bounced off the couch. She ran halfway across the room before she stopped and turned back to Penina. "Why?" she demanded.

"I think I still have that Sacagawea dollar in it," Penina answered. She hadn't promised to give Mimsy the dollar. She'd just mentioned that she thought it was in there.

Mimsy raced out of the room. Penina heard her going up the stairs—jumping up the stairs, it sounded like. Then she heard her come back down, banging the backpack on the steps behind her.

"Here's your backpack. Can I have my dollar?"

"Hold on. Sit down. Listen to this."

Mimsy sat. Penina found the notebook with her

139

half-finished letter to Ms. Anderson. She read Mimsy what she had so far, from "Dear Ms. Anderson" to "very much."

"So, what else should I say to her?" Penina asked. She found a sharpened pencil at the bottom of her backpack and turned to a clean notebook page.

"Why doesn't Ms. Anderson like Jews?" asked Mimsy. The idea that anyone anywhere might not automatically love her was clearly ridiculous.

"I'm not saying she doesn't. I'm just saying how she made me feel. She probably does like Jews. Actually, she probably doesn't even know any Jews, other than me and Ryan."

Mimsy moved up to sit on the back of the couch. She kicked her heels thoughtfully into the cushions. "I'm Jewish."

"I know." Mimsy was not a lot of help. If Penina ever did get over this flu, someday she would have to go back to school again. And she did not know what in the world she would say to her teacher when she got there. "Don't you have any idea what I should say to Ms. Anderson?"

Mimsy took a flying leap off the back of the couch. She landed like a gymnast, arms up, head back. Then she twirled, sat down like a pretzel, and said, "Invite her over for dinner, for Shabbat."

Penina put her head in her hands. Her sister was crazy, *meshugenah*. It sounded better in Yiddish, like, completely bonkers, off the wall. She couldn't invite Ms. Anderson for Shabbat. She would never come, and if she did come, no one would be able to enjoy any dinner because they'd have to talk about the metric system and state capitals the whole time.

"Do I get the golden dollar now?" asked Mimsy.

Penina held up her cup. It was tall and made of thick, bumpy green glass. It was very pretty, but it was empty, except for some melting ice and a chewed-on bendy straw. "Get me more orange juice first."

Mimsy just stood there.

Penina sighed, "Pretend you're a magic princess and you're bringing me a magic potion to break my spell. It's a coughing spell," Penina said, following up with a good, long cough.

Mimsy took the glass. She brought it to the bottom of the steps and yelled up, "Mom! Penina needs more orange juice."

Mom was there immediately, as if she had instantly materialized in the doorway. Penina hadn't even heard her walk down the steps. Maybe she had an advanced teleportation device. Or maybe Penina had been asleep during the time it took Mom to come downstairs and get her a drink.

"Here you go, honey. Sit up a little. Take a sip."

Penina sat and sipped. It wasn't orange juice. It was some kind of smoothie or something.

"It's orange–pineapple–kiwi–white grape. I invented it!" yelled Mimsy. She raised her pink plastic princess cup and took a long pull.

"It tastes like snot," Penina said. It didn't taste that bad, but Mimsy had to stop bragging about every single thing she ever did.

"Ah, that's the Penina we know and love," said Mom. She put her hand on Penina's neck. "You're cooling down. How are you feeling?"

"All right," Penina said. She took another sip of smoothie. It had actual bits of kiwi in it. It was really pretty good.

"Penina says she's going to die," Mimsy reported, like it was a crime to be sick or something.

Mom sat on the couch and put Penina's legs on her lap. "You're not going to die," Mom told her.

"Everybody dies," said Penina.

"You're not going to die this week," Mom promised. "You won't be done in by the common cold."

"But I have a fever," said Penina. "Maybe it's the flu."

"You're not going to die of the flu, either," said Mom. "I won't let you."

"What if I can't help it?" Penina asked. She didn't have a headache anymore. She felt comfy-cozy between Elgy and Mom. Mimsy climbed up and sat next to Mom, beside Penina's feet.

"If Penina dies, can I have her room?"

"Shh," said Mom, "she's not going to die. Dad is stopping on the way home to pick up something to make her feel better, an old family remedy."

Penina didn't know about any old family remedy. What was it? Chicken soup? Tea with lemon? That smelly stuff they rub on your chest?

"He's back!" yelled Mimsy. She sprang off the couch and zoomed to the front door. Penina turned onto her side. Dad came in with three big bags. Mimsy was jumping all around him. "What did you get, Daddy? What did you bring? Can I see it? Where did you get it? Is it heavy? What's that smell?"

"Hi, Pen. Hi, Sonia-leh," said Dad. He put the bags down on the coffee table. Mimsy reached inside one.

"Not so fast, Mimsykin," said Dad. "You don't want to spill this. Let me show you what we've got."

He began pulling small white cardboard cartons out of the bags. "Veggie lo-mien," he said. "Szechwan bean curd." He opened one of the cartons and took a whiff of the steam floating out of it. "Mmm, this must be the egg foo yung." He pulled out a plastic container as big as a carton of milk. "And, Penina," he said, "especially for you, so you should soon be back in the very pink of health, Hunan Special hot-and-sour soup!"

Penina smiled. They hadn't had take-out from Hunan since New Year's Day. "Thanks, Dad!" she started to say, but it came out as, "Th—*cough cough, cough.*"

But Dad knew what she meant. He patted her back as she coughed, and Mom held her hand.

Mimsy found the fortune cookies and broke one open. "Here's your fortune, Pina!" Mimsy shouted. She looked at the little piece of paper, even though she couldn't read. "It says, 'Mom and Dad and Mimsy and Daisy love you, so get well soon.'"

144

24. Love Rays

Penina didn't know much Hebrew, but she could say the blessing over wine along with everyone else: *"Bo-ray pree ha-ga-fen."*

She took a sip. Her wine was grape juice, sweet and cold and so purple it was almost black. Penina tucked in her lip so she would get a grape mustache when she drank it.

Penina looked around the table. Mimsy had a grape mustache. So did Zozo. So did Ryan.

Ms. Anderson did not.

"This wine is so good. It tastes just like grape juice," Ms. Anderson said, setting down her glass.

Dad, sitting next to Ms. Anderson at the head of the table, poured more wine into her glass. "Sweet wine for a sweet week," he said.

"Drink up," said Mom.

Ms. Anderson drained her glass. "Thanks. I better switch to grape juice now. I'll get dizzy."

Dad refilled her glass from the pitcher of grape juice.

Penina squinted at the Shabbat candles. They seemed to glow brighter when she squinched up her eyes.

"It was so nice of you to invite me for Friday night dinner. What's it called, again?"

"Shabbos," said Ryan.

"Shabbat!" yelled Mimsy.

"It depends on your accent," said Dad. He started a long story about languages and immigration and *blah blah blah.*

Ms. Anderson listened and smiled and ate two servings each of chicken, asparagus, rice, and challah —the special, sweet bread they had for Shabbat.

"I can't believe Ms. Anderson is sitting right here in my dining room," Penina whispered to Zozo.

"I can't believe you invited her," Zozo whispered back.

Penina couldn't believe it either. She hadn't meant to. It was Mimsy's fault. Penina had casually mentioned to Mom and Dad that she was thinking of inviting Ms. Anderson for dinner, and Mimsy had completely taken over. By the time Mimsy quit yelling that the whole thing had been her idea, and by the time Mom and Dad were done telling stories

of dinners they had been to when they were new teachers, and by the time everyone decided what would be on the menu and what they were going to wear and who else they would invite, there was no going back.

Penina invited Ms. Anderson for Shabbat dinner. She invited Ryan, too, so Ms. Anderson could eat with all the Jews in the class. She invited Zozo for moral support, and so she wouldn't have to tell her all about it later.

"This bread is awesome!" Ms. Anderson said. "My nana makes Swedish limpa bread. It's kind of like this, sweet and chewy."

"Is your nana Swedish?" Mom asked.

Penina didn't know if Ms. Anderson had brought anything to school for Diversity Days. What would it have been? Swedish meatballs? A Viking helmet?

"Maybe half. My family has everything: Swedish, German, Scots-Irish. And I guess when I have children, they'll be even more mixed up than I am," Ms. Anderson added.

When Penina was little, she used to think her teachers lived at school. Now, even though she knew teachers had lives and homes and families just like her parents did, it was hard to picture Ms. Anderson being a mother.

"That won't be for a while yet. I'm not even getting married till the middle of summer." Ms. Anderson looked dreamily into her glass of grape juice.

Penina raised her eyebrows at Zozo. Zozo raised her eyebrows back.

Mom clapped her hands. "Congratulations!" she said.

"*Mazel tov,*" said Dad. It was Hebrew for good luck, but they used it for *congratulations,* too.

"Yeah," said Ms. Anderson, "I can't believe it. When I go back to teaching next year, I won't be Ms. Anderson anymore. I'll be Mrs. Justin Jaworski."

"Justin Jaworski is a lucky young man," said Dad. He was overdoing the gracious-host thing a little bit, in Penina's opinion.

"I wish we had known. We would have invited him," said Mom.

"Oh, that's okay. He couldn't have come. He's in Singapore. He's a Lieutenant in the U. S. Army," Ms. Anderson said. Penina thought she heard her voice shake a little, but she might have been imagining things.

"Wow," Zozo whispered.

"Yeah," Penina whispered back. "Ms. Anderson has a boyfriend."

149

"More than that, a fiancé."

"More than that, a military *hero* fiancé."

"That must be very hard on you," said Mom. "I remember when David and I had to be apart, before we were married. I was in grad school, and David was offered a job at Ellsworth Elementary. . . ."

Zozo turned to Ryan and whispered, but not so softly that Penina couldn't hear it, "Sorry, Ryan. You can't marry Ms. Anderson after all. She's already engaged."

Penina thought Ryan would turn deep ruby red at that, but he just looked at Zozo and said, "That's okay. I'm saving up for a really big diamond, and then I'm going to propose to you, Zozo."

Penina almost snorted her grape juice across the table, she was so surprised. And Zozo did something Penina had never seen before. She blushed.

"Wow, Mimsy, that's great!" Ms. Anderson said. Mimsy had gotten up to stand beside the teacher's chair and was bragging about herself.

"And I can count to one hundred, and I can stand on my head," said Mimsy. She got into a tripod by the wall and kicked up into a headstand.

"Go, Mimsy!" Ms. Anderson yelled. "She is just adorable, Mrs. Levine."

"Thank you," Mom answered. She smiled at Mimsy,

and Penina could see her beaming love rays at her upside-down daughter.

Mom never beamed love rays at Penina. Penina got you're-grounded rays and pick-up-your-back-pack rays and what-did-I-ever-do-to-deserve-you-for-a-daughter rays. What would it take? What would Penina have to do to get a love ray look from her mother?

"Shabbat Shalom," said Daddy. Dessert was finished. The Shabbat candles were burned down to nothing. Dad held Ms. Anderson's jacket for her, and she slipped it on.

"Shabbat Shalom," said Ms. Anderson. "Hey, I'm speaking Hebrew." She smiled so much her teeth glittered. "Thanks for teaching me, Ryan,"

Ryan blushed.

"And thank you for inviting me, Penina," she said, and gave Penina a one-armed hug. It was quick and strong and had a friendly thump on the back at the end of it.

Dinner hadn't been so bad. Ms. Anderson was kind of nice. They should have her over again soon. Mimsy was right.

"It was Mimsy's idea," said Penina, and wished immediately she could take it back. What was she thinking? Now Mimsy would never stop bragging about her brilliant idea; the fabulous food; the wonderful centerpiece of home-grown daffodils and tulips; and how she, Mimsy, had thought of it, cooked it, arranged it, pretty much invented the whole idea of Shabbat dinner.

"It was both our idea," said Mimsy.

Penina stared at her little sister. Was this some kind of a trick? Some variation of the cuteness routine? Or was Mimsy really, for the first time ever in recorded civilization, sharing the spotlight with Penina?

Ms. Anderson knelt down and shook hands with Mimsy. "Well, thank you, Mimsy. I had a great time." Ms. Anderson stood up. "Mr. and Mrs. Levine, you have a wonderful family. You've got to be so proud of them."

"We are," said Mom. She turned to Penina and— Penina was 98 percent sure she wasn't seeing things—gave her a look. It wasn't exactly a love-ray look, but it was nice. It was like, *Good for you, Penina. You stayed true to your beliefs when Ms. Anderson asked you to write that Easter Bunny letter, and now you are reaching out to make peace with her. You are a principled person. We are proud of you, and we love you.*

Penina gave a look back. It was almost the same look, but it said, *Thank you. I know. I love you, too.*

"I'll see you Monday," Ms. Anderson said. She waved at Penina, Zozo, and Ryan, and then she went out to her car.

Ryan's father came to pick him up, and Penina's father walked Zozo back home.

Mom took Mimsy upstairs to help her wash up and put on pajamas.

Penina opened the back door and called, "Daisy!"

The cat came in, and Penina gave her some leftover chicken.

"Shabbat shalom," said Penina.

25. The Tenth Best Thing about Mimsy

"Barbara, look! It's a *conejote*. They must not be extinct after all!" said Penina-as-Barb.

Penina and Zozo watched a little brown rabbit (or a giant brown rabbit, if you were the size of Barb and Barbara) freeze beside the forsythia bush and then dash under the hedge at the back of Zozo's yard.

Conejotes, Penina and Zozo had decided long ago, were wild rabbits as big as horses. Their great herds had once roamed the remote wilderness where Barb and Barbara had their research station.

"We've got to document this sighting. That may be the last of its kind!" said Zozo-as-Barbara.

Barb and Barbara had lots of sophisticated photo equipment. Penina and Zozo had made it all from folded-up gum wrappers. But before Penina and Zozo could even help the naturalists on with their gear, Mimsy came tearing into camp, wearing the henin and toting her princess doll. "Mom said I could play with you!" she announced. "I brought Princess Miriam to play with your dolls."

"We're not playing dolls, Mimsy," Penina said. They weren't. It was hard to explain. Technically, Barb and Barbara were dolls, but the naturalists game was not dolly-dress-up. It was more like a real-world video game.

"It's role-playing," Zozo told Mimsy. "It's not for little kids."

"I'm not a little kid!" yelled Mimsy.

"We know you're not," said Penina. Sometimes agreeing with Mimsy was the quickest way to get her to stop screaming. "We're not . . . playing . . . dolls." Penina spoke slowly. She was making this up as she went along. "We're doing something else, and you can help."

Penina looked at Zozo to see if she minded. Who wanted to play with a four-year-old? Not Penina. But she didn't want to be grounded again, either, so running away from Mimsy or ordering her to leave them alone didn't seem like the best ideas.

Luckily, Zozo jumped right in. "Yeah, we're playing Truth-or-Dare."

"I'm the princess!" shouted Mimsy.

"There is no princess!" Penina shouted back.

Maybe she and Zozo should just hide in Zozo's room until Mimsy went away. How long would Penina be grounded for that? It might be worth it.

"It's not that kind of game," explained Zozo. It was easy for Zozo to be patient with Mimsy. She didn't have to live with her. "It's a game where you get to tell people what to do."

"Which makes it exactly like your real life," Penina added. Zozo chuckled a little, then explained the rules to Mimsy.

It was too itchy to sit in the grass, so they went up onto Zozo's back deck to play.

"You're youngest, so you can go first," Zozo told Mimsy. "Who do you want to ask?"

"You!" Mimsy pointed at Zozo and bounced around and giggled like a maniac.

"Okay, *dare*," said Zozo, and when Mimsy just kept bouncing and giggling, Zozo explained again. "Now you dare me to do something. Tell me something I have to do."

"Do six jumping jacks!" Mimsy commanded.

Zozo did them, the easiest dare in the history of the game.

"My turn," she said, tucking some loose hairs back into her crown braid. "Penina, truth or dare?"

"Truth." Penina hardly ever chose *dare*, especially

with Zozo. Zozo would make her go to school in her pajamas or talk pig Latin for a whole day. It was safer to choose truth. Zozo already knew everything about her anyway.

"Who do you love more, your mother or your father?"

"What?" That was a terrible question. There was no way to answer, and even if there were, Mimsy was sitting right there. She would report Penina's answer to the losing parent immediately. "That's not a real question. Pick a new one."

"Then it's a dare," said Zozo.

"Oh, come on. It's just you and me and my little sister. We don't have to go by the Official Truth-or-Dare Association of America rule book!"

"Okay, okay," said Zozo, "truth."

She didn't usually give in that easily, and by the time Penina realized why Zozo was being so agreeable, it was too late.

"What are the top ten things"—Zozo spoke in an extra-sweet voice, like a lady selling bubble-bath—"that you like about Mimsy?"

Penina gave Zozo a cold, evil look. *I'll get you for this. All the eyelash flutters in the world won't save you.*

Not that Zozo didn't try. Her lids looked like a mass migration of monarch butterflies. "Or, if you like, we could go back to dare," she said sweetly.

Mimsy looked back and forth between Zozo and Mimsy. It was the longest Penina had ever heard her be quiet.

Penina sighed. "Okay, fine. Ten things, but not in order." How was Penina going to think of ten good things about Mimsy? She couldn't even think of one.

Mimsy sat very still on the edge of the redwood bench she shared with Zozo. Her curly hair sproinged out in a crazy cloud beneath her henin—Penina's old pink henin.

"Well, she's good at recycling. If it weren't for Mimsy, that henin would be taking up room in a landfill by now."

"That doesn't count!" Mimsy yelled.

"Yes it does," said Zozo. "Mimsy, recycling is good. It means you're helping the environment."

Mimsy accepted that. One down, nine to go.

"She has nice eyes." Mimsy's eyes were big and brown. They took up a third of her face. Penina's sister was one of those round-eyed nocturnal animals, a kinkajou or something. "She, uh . . ." Penina stopped to think. This wasn't going to be easy.

"I let you borrow Elgy when you were sick!" said Mimsy.

"Yes, you did. Thanks. That's the third thing I like about you, Mimsy. You shared your bear."

With Mimsy's help, Penina got through five things in five seconds. Mimsy was good at making smoothies, she could jump down four steps at a time, she could count to one hundred, stand on her head, and sing all the words to *"Eliyahu Ha-navi."* (She had learned them since the Seder.)

"Sorry, Mimsy," said Zozo, "no fair helping. Penina has to do this all by herself."

"But those still count," Penina said. "I've got eight so far. Two more to go."

Too bad Penina couldn't use Mimsy's ideas anymore. Mimsy would have had no trouble coming up with the top 100 great things about herself. Penina stared at her sister, trying to read her mind. How would Mimsy answer the question?

"Remember," said Zozo, not-helpfully, "the question isn't just what Mimsy can do. It's what you *like* about her."

This was so unfair. Wait till it was Penina's turn. She hoped Zozo would pick truth. Penina would ask her something just as impossible. *What's it like not to have a father? Are all your supposed "food allergies" just an excuse for you to act oh-so-special?*

"There's a time limit," Zozo said.

"There is not. You can't just add a time limit in the middle of a question."

"I'm not. It's just that we are all going to have gray

159

hair and no teeth by the time you finish answering," said Zozo, and that made Mimsy giggle. Yeah, Zozo was hilarious.

"All right. I like how Mimsy . . ." *knows things.* She was like Zozo that way. They knew what to say to people, and how to say it. Neither of them would ever get sent to the LAC for swearing. ". . . how she keeps her cool."

"Really?" said Zozo. Even Mimsy looked surprised. Mimsy wasn't exactly a mellow kid, not what you would usually call *cool.* But Penina explained, and Zozo allowed it.

"Then tenth top thing I like about Mimsy is . . ." *Just say anything. Get it over with.* "She's my sister. We live in the same house. We have the same parents. She's one-fourth of our family." *One fifth, if you count Daisy.*

"Okay, stop. That's way more than ten!" said Zozo, no more sweety-sweet voice, Penina noticed.

Mimsy ran over to Penina and gave her a hug. "You're my sister, too, Pina!" she yelled.

Mimsy's hands were sticky, and the henin was poking Penina in the face. "Get off!" Penina said, and broke out of Mimsy's hug. "My turn, Zozo. Truth or dare?"

"No! Ask me!" screamed Mimsy. "I pick *dare!*"

"It's not your turn!" Penina screamed back. "It's mine, and I'm asking Zozo!"

"Ah, sisterly love," said Zozo, "how touching. Penina, just ask Mimsy one and then ask me. You'll get two turns."

"No. She can't just come in here and change the rules!"

"It's just you and me and your little sister," Zozo pointed out. "We don't have to go by the Official Truth-or-Dare Association of America rule book."

Mimsy looked victorious.

"Oh, all right. Mimsy, truth or dare?"

"Dare!" yelled Mimsy.

I dare you to be quiet for ten minutes. I dare you not to tattle for a day. I dare you to leave me alone for a week.

"I dare you to put your foot behind your head."

Mimsy did it. Little kids were rubbery. Penina used to be able to do that, too, but not anymore.

"Truth or dare, Zozo?"

"Dare," Zozo said. Of course. Penina should have known. Zozo always picked dare.

Penina tilted her head way back. She needed to think of a good one. She studied the blue sky and let her mind wander.

"Any day now," Zozo said.

"Zozo, I dare you to be Mimsy's sister for a day. For the next twenty-four hours, Mimsy lives with you, eats with you, plays with you. Until this time tomorrow, Mimsy is your little sister."

"Are you serious?" said Zozo.

Penina folded her arms. "It's a dare. Are you going to take it?"

"Yes!" Zozo yelled.

Mimsy bounced around the deck, shouting, "Goody goody goody. I get to sleep over at Zozo's!"

"Well, only if Mom says it's okay," Penina said. These two did not seem to be getting the point. This was a dare, not a celebration.

"She will! She will!" yelled Mimsy.

"And your mom, too, Zozo," said Penina.

Zozo raised her eyebrows. "Oh, please."

Penina remembered. Zozo's mom let her do any-thing she wanted.

"Here, Mimsy," said Zozo, "come in and call your mom and ask her if it's okay—Sis!"

"I'll ask," said Penina. "It's my dare." They went in, and Penina called her house. She didn't use the Window Phone, just the regular one in the kitchen.

She explained about the game and the dare. "But it is only on if you and Mrs. Miller say it's okay. You don't have to, though, because Mimsy's never been on a sleepover before, and she might get scared."

"Mimsy is almost five years old, and it's only right next door," Mom said. "I think she'll be fine. If it's all right with Mrs. Miller, it's all right with me. Let me talk to Mimsy."

Mom talked to Mimsy and to Mrs. Miller, and then to Mimsy again. Then Zozo got on the phone. Everyone was delighted about Zozo's new sister. What a splendid idea. What a fine time they would have. They'd pop popcorn and watch DVDs. They'd make jewelry with Zozo's hot-glue gun. In the morning, they'd go to Mass, and Mimsy could wear one of Zozo's old Sunday dresses.

"You're taking her to church?" asked Penina.

"You said till this time tomorrow," said Zozo. "Tomorrow is Sunday. I can't help it. It's your dare."

Penina had dared Zozo to be Mimsy's big sister for a day. Sisters went to church together. If Zozo could come to Shabbat dinner at Penina's house, then Mimsy could go to Mass with Zozo. She'd still be Jewish when she got back.

And in the mean time, Penina would have the house to herself. She'd have her parents to herself. The computer, the TV, the bathroom—*they will be mine, all mine!* Penina laughed like a greedy villain.

"What are you laughing at?" asked Zozo.

"Just planning my glorious sister-free day," Penina answered. This was going to be great. She and Mom would play backgammon. She'd get Dad to teach her how to knit. They'd go out for brunch, or maybe get takeout from Hunan.

And after that, Penina would probably call Zozo on the Window Phone and ask if she and her new sister wanted to come over and play.